LOST MINDS, WANDERING SOULS

VOL. II

A Collection of Short Horror Stories

By

GEORGE ADAMCZYK

George Adamczyk

TABLE OF CONTENTS

"Town Without Pity"

The brand-new day is beginning to peek through the window shades drawn at half-mast this morning. Barbara Adams stands like a flamingo at the stove, with her right foot on the ground, while the left is buried into her inner thigh. She smiles at a new song changing on her iPhone, playing on earbuds because her grouchy ass husband says he doesn't appreciate loud music in the morning. But honestly, it's that he doesn't appreciate her favorite music played loud in the morning. If she had been playing his favorite head-banging noise, he would tell her to turn it up. Another little compromise in the never-ending tug of war that is marriage.

The kitchen is sleek, charming, and upscale, a parallel of Barbara, who brightens the place as much as the sunshine. In stark contrast, gloomy Frank Adams slouches at the breakfast nook, a black cloud of negativity fogging up the atmosphere.

"Frank, if you're going to bring Paul over again tonight, you'd better stop after work and get more beer." Barbara says. "You two guys are two bottomless kegs."

"Huh? What? Oh, yeah, sure," answers Frank, who pushes his breakfast around on his plate the way a bored toddler would before making a half-hearted attempt to force it down. He used to love his wife's cooking, but now he can't seem to shake the Monday morning blahs that are starting to last all week. Frank groans as if a waiter had brought him sushi instead of a cheeseburger. His interest in food, and life in general, has crashed like the stock market during a recession.

He stares at her... pretty, spirited, and independent. She is wearing a short pink fuzzy robe which shows off the bottoms of the sexy tats meant only for him. Barbara resembles a bottle of champagne with the cork loosened till it's raring to pop, spreading cheer to everyone in the room. He would never blame her for the current soul-crushing rut he is in. He dug that himself with his own Alpha Male desires and, spoonful by spoonful, somehow made it seem as deep as the Grand Canyon.

Frank had been searching in vain for that elusive fulfillment he felt was missing in his heart, believing it would be his personal key to true happiness. But in the last several years, he came to the sad conclusion that everything in his world was close to perfect. He was merely being a narcissistic jerk. Still, something didn't feel right. No matter how hard he wracked his brain, he couldn't put his finger on it. It felt as if he had taken a wrong turn in life and driven himself right off the map.

Frank is already dressed for work, wearing the uptight executive suit and a tie that psychologically strangles him like a hangman's noose. He wishes he still had that enthusiasm that both he and Barbara once shared. Unfortunately, it was buried under all the drudgeries that adult life brings. It's as if a Google update messed up Frank's settings, and he was unwittingly switched into silent airplane mode. He shakes his head in disgust and buries his face into his phone. She turns and watches him with a tear that just won't drop out of her eye, as he flips from one app to the next in a futile attempt to wake himself out of his funk.

At 33, he's a successful executive and has the house, car, boat, and bank account to prove it. Everything that should make a young man happy. Yet somewhere along the line, he slipped into a desperate mental anguish that has latched onto him like a bear trap. Barbara sighs, heartbroken that he seems to have abandoned her for that sullen mistress named depression. Searching for any type of connection, she spots last night's lottery tickets on the windowsill. She saunters over with a glint of optimism, tossing them onto the table with a wistful smile.

"Here ya go, Sunshine." says Barbara. "Check the Powerball numbers. Maybe we won."

"Yeah, right," he grumbles, shoving the tickets aside.

"If winning 300 million dollars doesn't get you excited, I'm declaring you officially brain dead." exclaims Barbara.

"Then pull my life support, so I don't have to work anymore." he fires back. Her patience with his attitude wears thin.

"Well, if you're planning to sit around all night tonight watching sports, I'm going out with Ellen." Barbara responds.

"Whatever," declares Frank.

Their daughter, Caitlyn, pussyfoots into the kitchen, quiet as a mouse. She looks rather mousey as well: small, shy, and slouchy, with cropped, jet-black hair and a silver nose ring, drowning in an oversized Emo t-shirt. Her tiny paw slowly moves in to pinch a slice of French Toast from the frying pan without anyone spotting her. She hopes to scamper back to her den to nibble and avoid the drama-rama between her parents. But Caitlyn's mom is too sly for her. Barbara snatches Caitlyn by the wrist, without even turning around to see, with the expertise of a sorceress.

"CAITLYN. I thought we agreed you would eat breakfast at the table once in a while." yells Barbara.

"And I thought you guys agreed to stop bitching at each other once a month. So people could digest their food without wanting to run to the bathroom and throw up." says Caitlyn.

This final straw breaks Barbara's happy mood.

"See how this is affecting us? Your own daughter won't even eat a quick meal with us."

"I'm sorry, but the Brady Bunch was canceled 50 years ago. Not everyone can be as perfect as you are." Frank says.

"I'm not perfect... far from it. I used to think you were," responds Barbara. "It's like you're having your midlife crisis twenty years too early."

Caitlyn senses her chance and tiptoes around the creaks in the hardwood floor to escape the tortuous parental tirade. The sunshine disappears from Barbara's expression as she looks at his plate and notices Frank has hardly touched the breakfast she whipped up for him.

"What's wrong? You always loved my French Toast," Barbara says. "It's what I made you the morning after our after the first time."

Frank finally drags up the courage to look up at her. He wears the sad, drained face of a bloodhound who has lost his trail and honestly can't find it again.

"I know, Barbie, I know." agrees Frank.

"I don't understand why you're so miserable lately," Barbara wonders. "You've got me, and Caitlyn is such a sweetheart. She hides in her room or runs by her friends because you're so grumpy all the time."

"You're the best, and Caitlyn is the nicest daughter on the planet." says Frank.

"And pretty soon you're going to inherit the business. We'll have more money than we know what to do with." Barbara continues.

Frank leaps to his feet and goes into an animated tirade, flailing his arms in the air while circling the dining room.

"Oh, yes, Adam's Department Stores, my great grandfather's pride and joy." he barks and rolls his eyes in thinly veiled contempt. "Of course, he was proud. He came to this country with just the shirt on his back and worked like a dog until he saved enough money to build his store and helped build the surrounding town."

"Well, he did." shouts Barbara. "You've seen the old photos. Elmwood was just a church, a bar, and a stop sign until he…"

Frank callously interrupts her pleas.

"… brought jobs, prosperity, and a boon to the economy, and transformed Elmwood from a speck on the map to a thriving community that's still growing today." he says in a tone is as condescending as a slap in the face. All the sympathy and good intentions drain from Barbara's expression as if someone remotely lowered the brightness on her tv screen. She is finished trying to modify his sarcastic behavior. Snatching his breakfast plate from the table, she angrily scrapes her delicious meal into the trash.

"You realize sarcasm is not an art form the way you try to make it." says Barbara.

"If it was, I would be a regular Van Gogh." Frank spouts out with a smug look on his face as if he thinks he's won a sort of spousal competition.

"Well, I am so sorry for chewing your ear off." she one-ups him.

Frank pops himself in the chest, comically taking an arrow to the heart.

"And Barbara, once again, for the win." he says.

Barbara turns around in disgust, boiling over in frustration, precisely as her organic oatmeal boils over on the stove. She rushes to turn down the heat and clean up the mess. Frank realizes he took the sparring repartee one step too far.

"I am so sorry, honey." he contends. "I just feel so trapped in that place."

"Nobody forced you to work in the family business." says Barbara.

"No, just pushed, prodded, threatened with ex-communication." Frank answers.

Barbara attempts to switch her approach and charm him back to contentment.

"But you used to love it there. Why all of a sudden do you act as if it's a Nazi death camp?" she wonders.

"It got to the point where I feel as if I'm living someone else's dream. Of course, I'm proud of what he accomplished, but I'm just another wheel in the cog." Frank professes. "I've worked my butt off and made a ton of money for the business, but where is my glory? Where are my dreams?"

Barbara's eyes melt with pure empathy radiating from them, and she takes Frank's hand in hers.

"Well, what is it you want to do with your career?" she asks. "I'll help you; I'll back you up every step of the way."

Frank sinks back into the kitchen chair, a defeated bag of weary bones.

"I don't have a clue. How can I, when I've been eating, breathing, and sleeping that place my entire existence?" he says with all the sadness of a dyslexic kid who can't figure out why he can't read.

"Millions of people hate their jobs, and they don't change into sulking heaps of despair." Barbara says.

"I know, but whenever I'm in the office and I see that humongous portrait of him glaring down at me, it's like, he built something. He changed people's lives." Frank responds.

"You changed my life." Barbara professes.

"And you changed mine. But that store envelops me, sucks out my soul." Frank says. "Makes me feel that Jonathan Adams was a great man full of adventure. And Frank Adams will never be anything but a suit and a bank account."

Although Frank's depression is sincere, and his dreams are worth consideration, his vain complaints spread across the room like an unwelcome fart. Barbara sees there is nothing she can do short of physically kicking him in the ass to change his attitude. He slumps in his chair into his private oblivion. So, she slinks away in silence to her music and oatmeal.

Frank wallows in his swamp of self-pity for a few moments. A silent alarm goes off in his head, signaling it was time to leave. He slugs down his coffee as if it were some type of medicine he needed to take, grabs his keys, and heads for the door.

"I gotta go," he says.

"Go, spread that unique brand of Frank Adams melancholy around the world." Barbara fires back.

Frank opens the door to walk out, but lingering guilt compels him to turn back to apologize once more. It's too late, however. He only catches a glimpse of Barbara's cute pink butt as she wanders around the corner into the next room. Angry that he missed his chance, Frank slams the door behind him. Barbara softly chuckles to herself, wondering if she would ever stop hoping for a goodbye kiss. It had been months since Frank kissed her before going to work. Yet she still feels that spark of expectation every morning. Only to see it crash and burn as he squealed out of the driveway.

Surly Frank is marooned in his own private hell, too out of it to notice. He drags himself to his car in a daze. Outside is a typical suburban street, with impeccable landscaping and sparkling sidewalks, sickeningly sweet in its perfection. Neighborhood kids in uniforms and backpacks parade to school in platoons, marching off to war. SUVs are like Army jeeps on maneuvers, carrying mothers, babysitters, and carpoolers instead of military personnel. Frank has witnessed this preppie panorama countless times but still lets out an involuntary gag.

"This is supposed to be Elmwood, not Stepford." he grumbles to himself.

He gets into his car, a brand new sporty red Lexus Barbara got him for his birthday. She hoped the gift would cheer him up, but that only worked for a few weeks before he returned to his old grumpy self. Frank speeds off past the monotonous malls and cookie-cutter corporate buildings that strangle every suburb out of any hope of uniqueness. Every corner seems to have a "Morebuck's Coffee" or a "Goofy Glaze" donut shop.

Different excuses pop into his head with each passing intersection. Frank just can't figure out why he feels miserable all the time. Sure, he had fantasized about quitting the family business and finding a more exhilarating profession... porn star, marijuana farmer, or maybe government assassin. In truth, his job wasn't really that bad. Staff meetings and marketing strategies were not exactly a thrill a minute. But he had a beautiful house and family to come home to. Softball games, fishing trips, and weekend barbecues... how could he ask for anything better?

He thought he was merely bipolar or had one of those myriad forms of depression they show on so many TV commercials. It was as if they kept making up new varieties to sell expensive medications for. Yet prescriptions only masked the problem, and it returned with a vengeance whenever he weaned himself off them. Maybe it was the drive to work. Talk about monotonous. Hang a right on Monroe Street, then cutting in and out of traffic so methodically, he could practically do it blindfolded.

Frank realizes in this town, the more things changed, the more they've stayed the same. Slurpee-faced kids in front of the 7/11, middle-aged ladies dragging their reluctant husbands off to go shopping, and the same people driving the same cars to the same jobs, every... single... day. The sun is bright, the sky is blue, the air is clear; it's all so perfect, it makes him sick.

8

Frank has lived here his entire life. His great grandfather was the president and founding member of the town's original Chamber of Commerce. Elmwood grew from a speck on the map to a thriving city in several generations. Frank felt himself getting stale here. His deepest desire was to make his own mark in life somewhere, somehow. He just couldn't find time out of his vicious circle of work and home life to figure out how. He wracked his brain, but nothing he ever came up with sounded right. The thought of all his lost hopes and dreams made him bang his fist on the outside of the car door.

He converges on the upwardly mobile downtown section of Elmwood. Expensive stores owned by conglomerates from out of state, featuring all the latest fashions and fads. Pretentious restaurants with prices gouged up just high enough to scare away the common residents considered undesirable by the corporate moguls.

And here is "Adam's", formerly "Adam's Five & Dime", the store that launched a dynasty. His great grandfather's pride and joy. The women's fashions now displayed in the massive row of windows were probably making him roll over in his grave. Obscenely flashy patterns and scandalously designed outfits that didn't cover enough flesh to be used as underwear in his day. Not in this section of the country. This is the shining jewel of his family's dynasty. The flagship store, rebuilt over the site of the original. The first of dozens to follow in the tri-state area. But to Frank, it felt like his graveyard.

Suddenly, things start getting blurry. He rubs his eyes and blinks repeatedly, but his vision keeps getting worse. What really freaks him out is… only certain things are blurred… everything else is crystal clear. Frank is so stunned that he slows his car to a crawl.

"What the frack is going on?" he wonders.

The store becomes foggy and seems to be fading, yet the sky and scenery behind it are perfectly normal. And the clothes on the mannequins appear to be… changing.

"Holy sh…."

His expletives are drowned out by the screeching of tires as he slams on his brakes. He lunges forward a little as a result and catches a glimpse of the rearview mirror. The car speeding behind him is on

9

the verge of colliding into his. He braces for the impact, as for whatever reason, the other car isn't even slowing down. He clenches his teeth and squints his eyes but feels nothing. There is no impact whatsoever. How is that possible?

He sees that as the other vehicle reaches him, it begins to fade. The transparent ghost car passes right through his. Then it glides through Frank himself. It continues past unabated, only to completely vanish thirty feet in front of him. Frank's jaw drops, his forehead falls to the steering wheel, and his hands slide off, hanging limp at his sides. At that moment, there is a numb pause in his life. His entire consciousness goes blank. Everything taken for granted in life... death, taxes, dirty politicians, and morons on the internet... all take a flying leap out the driver's side window. He lets his foot slide off the brake pedal, and the car idles into the curb.

Frank might have stayed that way for a long time but for the cigarette in his hand burning his finger and shocking him back to reality. He flicks it out the window, wearing the empty glare of a man who had been instantly lobotomized. Outside, things are still changing.

"What the hell is going on?" he asks himself.

He gropes his way out of the car and stumbles to the display windows. The glass and granite facades are getting hazier and harder to make out. The colors of the clothes are changing, swirling from bright, psychedelic tints to basic blacks, whites, and blues. Inexplicably, the garments themselves start transforming, from floppy rap star gear and elegant evening wear into common shirts and bib overalls. His hands, sweaty and shaking, streak across the glass as he staggers.

"This is insane." he contends.

Frank has rushed right by a mental breakdown and teeters one step away from certifiable insanity. In an instinctive urge of self-preservation, he squeezes his eyes shut and tightens his fists, as if he's hanging for dear life onto a rope swaying over a bottomless pit. Gasping in quivering heaves, he tries to work himself into a calmer state by taking slow, deep breaths. Perhaps he should have gone with Barbara when she asked him to attend yoga classes with her.

Trying to get his head straight, Frank snaps his head and shoulders back like a soldier coming to attention. He combs his hair back with his hands and finds he can finally exhale a breath without trembling. He opens his eyes once more, hoping desperately to find it was but a bad dream. Only the scene is getting worse. Now the entire building has changed from a slick slate exterior to dirty old bricks. Its height has reduced from three stories of shopping mall perfection down to 14 feet of country-style quaintness. Huge sections of the store have utterly vanished. And the sign has switched from "Adam's" to "Sale-Mart".

"No. This can't be happening," he yells.

Frank rushes frantically up the street, his head spinning as his world transforms around him. As his footsteps click along, the pavement changes from black asphalt and yellow-painted lines to cracked, faded concrete. Suddenly, a filthy antique gas station inexplicably erupts from the blacktop, appropriating half of the store's parking lot.

In a panic, he runs blindly into the middle of the street and finds himself dodging traffic. A car horn blares. He turns to see it swerve just barely enough to avoid pulverizing him, then abruptly disappear into nothingness. A brand-new green Nissan Cube parked a few feet away transforms into a beat-up old red pickup truck. A huge dent instantly emerges on another vehicle right in front of his eyes. A minivan materializes out of nowhere. A large school bus crammed with kids shrinks into a short bus carrying only a handful.

"No. No. No, get this nonsense away from me." Frank screams.

And the insanity continues. He lunges across the street. There lies Le Francais, the hot new French restaurant where the up-and-coming young execs flash their jewelry and Gold Cards and nibble on incredibly designed but insanely priced entrees. He watches in near hysterics as it melts down into the dingy diner "Apple Pie Annie's." Even more bizarre, the well-groomed clientele inside mutates into dusty truckers with three days of stubble carpeting their faces. The BMWs and Mercedes parked in the valet area mold together to form road-worn Mack and REO trucks with out-of-state license plates.

Frank whirls around, but everywhere he looks, things are changing, disappearing, or metamorphosing. As a guy with a man-bun approaches, it unravels and his dyed blond hair fades to brown. His clothes turn from urban casual to jeans and a flannel as he walks past. And he doesn't even notice.

"What's going on? Do you know what's going on?" he asks. But the man acts as if Frank isn't even there. He tries to grab another guy and force him to listen, but his hands pass right through the man's chest. Frank crumples into a trembling heap upon the rapidly deteriorating sidewalk.

"This can't be happening." he exclaims.

He tries closing his eyes to shut off all these impossible events. He attempts to explain to himself how he could be witnessing the uncreation of an entire suburb. Did he accidentally ingest some bad acid? Were all the tinfoil hat conspiracy theorists correct, and the CIA was crop-dusting the country with evil chemtrails? But that simply pushes him further past the brink, so he reluctantly peels them back open. Directly ahead is an older woman shuffling towards him. He recognizes her and leaps to his feet.

"Mrs. Vorchek. Mrs. Vorchek." Frank shouts.

The familiar face of his high school science teacher, who loved baking, growing vegetables, and sending him to the principal's office, emerges from a crowd of pedestrians. The nervous ache in the pit of Frank's stomach melts away when her bespectacled eyes start to recognize him. A discerning smile warms her weary, errand-running expression. He races towards her, heart in his throat. He screams her name with an unbelievable sense of reassurance, as if a terrible guilt has somehow been lifted from his soul. It certainly looks as if she sees him, and her lips move as if she's about to say his name. The color of relief returns to his pale face with every step he takes.

"Thank God, I saw you, Mrs. Vorchek." Frank says.

But to his horror, she begins to squint, with a perplexed look in her eyes. As if the thought of him had simply faded away from her memory. Her attention drifts, and she turns back to window shopping as if she had never seen him. Frank stretches out to touch her, his last link to reality, but can only grasp a wisp of a spectral vision as she abruptly vanishes. Frank spins around and searches everywhere, but the lady is MIA.

Tears and sweat pour out of him as if he's standing in the rain, but his mouth is a desert. His heart beats like someone just dropped the bass, his stomach throbs like an abused punching bag, and his eyes roll around in their sockets as if he is in a cartoon. He bites his lip till it begins to bleed, while things around him continue their transmutations with no reasonable explanation.

He races away blindly, dodging pedestrians like would-be tacklers on a football field until he turns a corner. Another man is jogging towards him from the opposite direction, and Frank barrels right into him. The collision should have knocked them both down for the count. Yet they pass right through each other like ghost ships in the night fog. Frank hardly misses a beat, as he spins around and speeds onwards, trying in vain to ignore that people's clothes are changing right on their bodies, and the bodies themselves are changing from thin and fit to plump and happy.

"Make this stop, please," yells Frank.

Was he dead? Was he killed when that car plowed into him on Monroe? Was this purgatory? Or hell? Could he be traveling back in time? This certainly isn't the Elmwood he knew. Some of the newer businesses have been replaced by older ones he remembered from his youth or had heard about years ago from family and friends. He was watching as his entire hometown was antiquing itself.

Out of the blue, he spots a place that makes him stop dead in his tracks. Just ahead is an old-fashioned shot-and-beer joint that hasn't changed in decades. Ralph's Tavern has been a staple in Elmwood since well before Frank was born. A place where everyone feels welcome, from the newly arrived urban transients to the folks whose families have lived here since the entire area was farmland and dirt roads. A place that never ages or loses its charm, running like a trolling motorboat over a glassy lake through whatever societal havoc each generation creates, decade after decade. And it isn't changing at all.

He makes a mad dash for his favorite dive, hoping desperately to find some sort of salvation there, not even concerned as a commuter bus drives right through him. He leaps up the curb and reaches for the knob. But his hand passes right through it. Frustrated, he squares his shoulders and strides right in through the solid wooden door.

Inside, it is as cool and dark as a basement during football season. He stands at the entrance for a moment and smiles. Little, if anything, has changed. And nothing is blurring, swirling, or reinventing itself. Old Pabst and Schlitz signs that now qualify as antiques line the walls, along with sports pennants and ads for toaster oven pizza and beef jerky. The welcome sounds of pings and bells signal that someone is playing the old pinball machine in the corner. The smell of stale beer and decades-old sweat permeates the atmosphere.

Frank once thought he would walk in and find these same guys sitting on those same barstools, but as skeletons covered with cobwebs. Then he remembers all the nights that he closed this dump instead of going home to Barbara and Caitlyn. He should probably have his name engraved in bronze on the corner stool. The smile falls off his face as if he had dropped his phone in the toilet.

But there is Harry, the blustery red-headed bartender who ran the joint. A street-smart guy who truly enjoys the simple life, and the hearty smile that proved it rarely left his lips. Even when bum-rushing town drunks out the door after fistfights that only their dentists would smile about. He's serving tap beers to his early morning patrons as classic rock plays on the jukebox.

"Yes. I love you, Ralph's. Nothing ever changes here." Frank says. He dries his face with his sleeve and approaches the bar with a weary smile.

"Hey Harry, do you know what the heck is going on?" he asks. But he gets no response. The uneasy sensation that his favorite bartender refuses to acknowledge him eats away at Frank's newfound happiness.

"Harry, please tell me you can see me." he yells.

Harry walks away to serve the other customers, and Frank follows like a puppy who needs attention.

"Harry? Pete? Jose? Please tell me I'm not going crazy." Frank exclaims.

He tries to get control of himself. This is the one place he feels comfortable. A place where he can think. Did the car crash kill him? But then why were things changing? Even if he had died, the town should stay the same. Did his mind snap? Was this his final escape from the reality he had come to despise? He spots an unattended bottle of bourbon on the bar and swipes at it, but it is like swishing his hand through a hologram.

"Oh God, no." he says.

Now Frank is more freaked out than ever. He staggers to the center of the bar, mumbling incoherently.

"I gotta get outta here... I gotta get outta here... I gotta get outta here."

His stammering gets louder and louder until he explodes, swinging his fists at everything within reach, yet connecting with nothing but vodka-scented air. He bolts for the exit, a maniac escaping the asylum. But right as he is ready to storm out, something catches his eye. Halfway in and halfway out of the doorway, he spots a framed photo on the wall.

"The team." he remembers.

On the wall is a poster-sized picture of the bar's softball team. It calms Frank a little at first, seeing an object that reminds him he is still alive. That he is still a part of reality. But then his demeanor flips like a switch on a jailhouse electric chair.

"What the hell is this? I should be in this photo." Frank shouts.

He peers over it like a Where's Waldo, trying to find his face where it was supposed to be, among his best friends. But it is nowhere to be seen. His anger surges like a volcano ready to erupt. His finger slides along the photo, up and down, back and forth, over and over.

"I should be right here." Frank says. "Wait a damn minute. Paul Lucas? He's not on the team. He barely made the practice squad."

But there was no doubt. The face of his best buddy Paul was in the photo. In fact, it was exactly where Frank's face should have been. The captain of the team had been replaced by a scrub off the bench. Frank charges to the bar, furious over being erased from the poster.

"Why ain't I on the team photo? What did you guys do with the real one?" he questions.

No one responds, so Frank raves even louder.

"I can't believe you guys. Harry? Pete? Jose, why won't you listen to me?" he cries. He storms back to glare at it again, so angry that he tries in vain to rip it from the wall. Now practically deranged, he tries to rationalize what is occurring by assigning blame.

"Paul Lucas. He was always jealous of me. I could tell." Frank contends. "I was always better than him at everything. I was a better athlete, better looking, better with women."

He rambles at the guys at the bar as if he thinks they can hear him, getting more and more irrational by the second.

"And he works at that weird government lab, where everything is so hush-hush all the time. They may have found a way to steal a person's life, erase them from existence." Frank says. His eyes pop wide as if he's made a huge discovery.

"Steal their life? Steal their WIFE. Paul was always crazy about Barbara." he continues. The song on the jukebox ends with a scratch. Frank can now hear what his friends at the bar are saying, and it isn't good. The always happy Harry sounded increasingly like a mortician at a funeral.

"It's a shame, a real damn shame," Harry mourns.

"They were such nice people. They were always fun when they stopped in here." Pete laments.

"Yeah, Barbara was a great lady. And he was cool, too." Jose replies.

"What about Barbara? What do you mean... was?" Frank asks.

He turns up to the television set where everyone's eyes are transfixed. The news is showing firemen standing around a burnt-out building that looks eerily familiar. The reporter continues with her story.

"... witnesses say that the extra-alarm blaze tore through the home on James Street in mere moments and that the owners had no chance to escape." the reporter says.

Frank stares at the smoldering remnants of the house in sheer horror. What little remains of the home appears to be the house that Frank had left less than half an hour earlier.

"James Street? That looks the same as my house. Before we did the renovations. This can't be. Barbara? Caitlyn?" he says.

Frank hurdles through the bar door like a bat out of hell. Outside, Elmwood has transformed from a massive commercial development into a small town "Main Street" that Andy Griffith would be proud of. But Frank doesn't notice. There is only room for a single thought in his mind. He speeds up the street, desperate to return to a home and a reality that may no longer exist. He turns the corner to the store, but his car is no longer where he left it.

"Damn." Frank shouts.

There is no time to come up with alternate plans. Without a second thought, Frank turns around and sprints full speed towards home. His strides get longer and longer, but he doesn't notice. His breathing is as rhythmic as an Olympic sprinter, but he couldn't care less. He is on a mission now, to go back and find his family who he never truly appreciated. The family he ignored whenever he was home and whined about whenever he wasn't. Everything is going to change now. He is going to be the best husband ever, Father of the Year.

Nasty memories zip by with each passing block. The time he forgot to attend Caitlyn's soccer championship. The time he went to play golf instead of celebrating Barbara's promotion. Never again, he tells himself. Everything will be perfect from now on. Just let me get back to my old existence. Back to the family that I love more than life itself. Please let...

He turns the last corner onto James Street, and there is his house. "Was" is the correct term, for it is unrecognizable. All that remains are the few skeletal charcoal black beams and 2 x 4's studs of a burnt-out shell. It is scorched to the foundation, as is Frank's soul. The weight of his entire world collapses onto his shoulders, knocking him to his knees with an agonizing thud. He kneels there on the ground for what seems like eons... panting, shattered, lost. Is this where you beg for forgiveness? Is this where you pray for another chance? Where are Barbara and Caitlyn? They must still be alive. They can't be...

Suddenly, something whizzes right through him, a newspaper. It is tossed by a grief-stricken kid pedaling his mountain bike slowly past the grim scene. Frank crawls towards it, through the soggy ashes that were once his home. It appears slightly different. Smaller, thinner than their regular local newspaper. But that doesn't matter. The bold headline cuts like a knife through his heart.

"LUCAS FAMILY DIES IN TRAGIC FIRE"

Underneath are photos of Barbara, Caitlyn, and Paul Lucas. Frank is horrified as he reads the article below.

"The town of Elmwood is in mourning today, as Paul Lucas, his wife Barbara, and daughter Caitlyn were killed in a terrible fire in the early morning hours of..."

"What the hell is going on? Barbara is my wife. Caitlyn is my kid. Lucas, you son of a bitch."

Frank's mind spins around in madness. Paul had somehow taken over Frank's life, his entire existence. But how? He finally starts to doubt his sanity. None of this is possible in the real world. Not even the CIA could arrange anything this bizarre. His chronic boredom has blossomed into full-blown psychosis. He rolls around on the ground as if his face has splashed with acid. His sanity is stretched beyond the breaking point.

"No. No. No. No." he cries. Suddenly, he hears a robotic voice from out of the blue.

18

"Frank Adams."

Frank snaps to his feet in a flash, the way a predator does when it senses an enemy preparing to attack. A figure enters this reality from a colorful, glowing slash in the atmosphere. It is a somber form silhouetted in the brilliant morning sun, dressed in a jet-black bodysuit that covers all but his face. His face is stoic, seemingly ageless as an ancient Greek statue, and even more profound. His features are handsome, yet plastic, robotic. Frank rushes to confront him yet stops warily a few yards away. The anger in his eyes mix with a bit of fear for this stranger.

"You know me? You can see me?" Frank asks although he knows they are stupid questions as soon as they leave his lips. "How do you know who I am? What's happening here?"

"I have tracked you down to explain. I am from your future. I was experimenting with a device that you might categorize as a time machine, researching the era 50 years before your own. When I traveled to a street corner that was supposed to be deserted according to all our sensors, I found it wasn't. A man was standing there, and he saw me appear out of nowhere. I approached and tried to calm him, but I failed to make him understand what had happened. He ran and hid in a place where I could not find him or reason with him."

Frank approaches closer, getting surly, not liking what he is hearing.

"I had no other choice but to return to my own time and try to correct the error. I discovered through ancient records that because of the unfortunate incident, many events that should have taken place never occurred. The man was shocked so severely that he doubted his sanity and it shattered his confidence. He never married, never moved here to Elmwood, never helped build this community. That man was your great-grandfather."

All of Frank's insanity and overwhelming guilt transforms into a surge of sheer outrage. He bolts up and gets right in the man's face. But the heat from Frank's anger and frustration has no effect on his cold expression.

"So, you're telling me that this is your fault? You screwed up my entire life? You bastard. I'll kill you."

Frank puts all his energy a haymaker punch that should have knocked the man back to the future. But the figure vanishes before he can connect and reappears behind him.

"Please do not attempt violence again. I can move through time and space and avoid your every attack. It would be futile and vulgar."

Frank steps away to regain control of his faculties. He realizes he can't hurt the guy, and he never really wanted to, anyway. It was the instinctive reaction of a frustrated man under extraordinary circumstances. But that doesn't mean he isn't still mad as hell. He angrily points his finger at the man like he's holding a gun, acting as threatening as possible.

"Listen, whoever you are. You gotta fix this. You ruined my life and the lives of everyone I care about. What is all this, anyway? Am I dead or what?"

"You are in what best can be described as a time limbo. You are not dead, for now. It is as if you were never truly alive. Since you did have an existence, your soul remains, but without a body. Because in the way I altered time, your body was never actually created. A soul is made of energy, which can never die. So, you are here, in this town, where you should have lived if your ancestor had fulfilled his destiny."

Frank's face pales with incomprehension.

"So now what's gonna happen?"

"I spent countless hours tracking your every movement, and finally was able to tell you the truth before you lost your grip on your sanity. I will go back now to attempt to rectify the situation. It will be extremely difficult. I have to arrive at the precise moment your relative spotted me, then distract his attention so he never witnesses my first arrival." the man says.

"You mean it will be like this never happened? Everything will return to the way it was?" Frank asks.

"Yes. If I am successful, you will know it in an instant. Your life will be restored as you remember it. This will be a nightmare that will dissipate from your consciousness. Sorry is the most useless word in your prosaic language, so I will instead apologize by restoring you to your proper life. Farewell, Frank Adams."

And, with that, the Man in Black is gone.

"WAIT. I need to know..." Frank has a million questions he wants to ask, although in that frantic moment he can't think of one. Maybe the Man in Black knew explanations were a waste of time. Frank attempts to comprehend all he's been through. Hopes this nightmare will soon be forgotten. He lets out the biggest sigh of relief in his life. Whatever happened, whatever insanity this was, the Man in Black said he was going to return it to normal. He would get his life back, and never, ever take Barbara or Caitlyn or anything for granted again.

He finally realizes that nobody starts from scratch. Everyone builds on what others have done before. Jonathan Adams didn't worry about lofty goals or some elusive secret to happiness. He simply got up every morning and worked his butt off, trying to make things better a little better than the day before.

But seconds pass into minutes. Minutes pass into hours. The Man in Black had said that, if he were successful, Frank should know it instantly. What kind of future will he have if his past never truly existed?

The brand-new day is just beginning to peek through the window shades drawn at half-mast this morning. Barbara Adams stands like a flamingo at the stove, with her right foot on the ground, while the left is buried into her inner thigh. She smiles at a new song playing on her iPhone and turns the volume to full blast because her loving husband loves hearing her music in the morning.

Her husband Paul is a reserved but charming guy, the Yang to her Yin. Medium height, medium weight, medium looks. The only thing he was above average at was being perfect for Barbara. And being a great husband. He sneaks up from behind her and gives her a seductive hug and kiss on the neck. Barbara lets out a sexy growl and turns to cuddle him back. Paul takes her by the hand and twirls her, dancing her across the room. He stops and pulls her tight, dips her down, and showers her with a barrage of kisses.

"Do we really have to go to work today? Can't we call in sick?" Barbara laughs.

"Oh, no. Not again. Do I have to be exposed to this every morning?" Caitlyn giggles as she strolls in for breakfast. She's now a slinky sweet ball of energy, wearing an Elmwood High School softball team t-shirt, with wavy purple hair and a smile that energizes any room she walks into. Her parents manage to get themselves untangled long enough to drag her into a silly but heartfelt group hug.

"Hahaha, okay, okay. As much fun as this is, I gotta go to work." says Paul, extricating himself from the clutches of his two favorite ladies.

"Alright, but don't think you're going to get away this easy tonight when you get home." Barbara says.

"I can't help it I'm so irresistible to women." Paul replies.

"You are." Barbara and Caitlyn spout out in unison, laughing as they high-five each other, while Paul shakes his head in amusement.

"Caitlyn, do you want to drive to school with me or are you riding there with your friends?" Barbara asks.

"No, Mom, I'll go with you."

Paul opens the door for his girls, who head to Barbara's car. All wave their goodbyes to each other as they drive off. Paul turns right towards his lab, and the girls head in the opposite direction.

Barbara and Caitlyn engage in typical mother-daughter banter as the blocks flow past. They don't appear to recognize that this is a different Elmwood. It is not the affluent, almost smug suburb that Frank had helped build, nor is it the rustic rural community of his hallucinatory nightmare. It is somewhere comfortably in between. Frank actually had made a difference, even though he never recognized it. They gab and giggle joyously, another in an endless string of happy, precious moments that they've been having since Caitlyn was old enough to go to school.

But both go silent, as an eerie sensation envelops them. As they pass the recently renovated Sale-Mart Super Store, the ghostly apparition of Frank Adams materializes out of nowhere. He gives one last heartbreaking wave to them from the corner sidewalk as their car rolls past. And like the last puff of cigarette smoke from a dying cancer patient, he evaporates forever into the time limbo that he will haunt for eternity.

Barbara loses control of her car and squeals to the curb, narrowly avoiding a serious collision with several parked cars, her face pale and petrified.

"Mom, who was that?" Caitlyn cries.

"You saw him, too?" Barbara asks. They b... t... gaze through the rear windshield, frantically searching, but the spectral figure is gone.

"Yes, he was like a ghost. Who was that, Mom? He seemed so familiar."

Barbara bursts into uncontrollable tears and Caitlyn can't help but begin bawling herself.

"I DON'T KNOW. I don't know who he was." she wails.

"Why are we crying? Why are we so sad?" Caitlyn screams.

"It's...it's like I should know him. It's like...a part of me, a part of my life just...vanished."

They squeeze each other tight, crying in near hysterics, mourning the loss of a man whom they once loved in another life. A man who now never actually existed.

"Evil

Reincarnate,"

An ominous voice resonates over the P.A. system through the halls of a sparkling new hospital wing.

"Code Blue, Room 307. Code Blue, Room 307."

The swinging doors of a huge room burst open. An extra complement of nurses and doctors rush into the already crowded suite.

They roll in strange medical equipment, squeezing them between other life monitoring devices which are bleeping and flashing like slot machines in Las Vegas. This is not your normal, everyday Intensive Care Unit. This is the ICU of the Rich and Famous. Luxurious hospital care that only the richest 1% of humanity will ever see. The most honored physicians in their fields. The latest, most expensive technology. Yet they are fighting a losing battle. The lingering smell of death and disinfectant pervades the atmosphere.

Despite all their hard work and cutting-edge technology, Jackson Morgan is going to die.

He began amassing his fortune with common thievery and petty larceny. His dishonesty grew exponentially, inventing vicious stock market schemes that even seasoned traders found reprehensible. He soon had everything any man could ever desire, multiplied by a thousand. Yet everything was never good enough for this insatiable monster. He is wealthy to the obscene yet plays the part of an aristocrat with the authenticity of a community theater actor. His table manners were crude, his language vulgar. He was nouveau riche, crawling from the gutters as a deadly snake, invading the gardens of high society. It was there he found his true calling, becoming a card-carrying member of the 1%. That inhumanely greedy group of sociopaths who thrive on plundering every penny from the working class. He spent his leisure hours watching the brutal suffering it caused with merciless glee.

Now his sordid existence hangs by a thread. Dr. Ericson, an intense physician with a permanent crinkle between his benevolent blue eyes, strides in and takes command of the situation. The exasperation on his face reveals the fact he never wanted to be here. He had declined a multitude of exorbitant offers to take over Morgan's healthcare. Until his employers received an irresistibly excessive bribe. Ericson was coerced to accept the position, or they would force his resignation and comfy a permanent black mark on his resume.

It wasn't that Ericson was unsympathetic to Morgan's plight. Even though the multi-billionaire had once placed second on a survey of the most hated man in history. Right behind Adolph Hitler. It was because Morgan was a lost cause from the beginning. Having him as a patient was like patching holes in a boat made of Swiss cheese. No matter what they did, he was going to sink. And stink. He already has the smell of an old serial killer victim dug out of a molding crawlspace. Ericson and his entire team knew going in that no matter what they tried, their privileged patient is five minutes from a cold date with the coroner.

"What have we got, Sheila?" he asks.

Sheila is the head critical care nurse, a tiny ginger fireball. A no-nonsense veteran of countless life-or-death battles, her batting average for keeping patients alive is considered the best in the business. Unceremoniously snatched from her dream job at a cutting-edge hospital for sick children and forced to preside over this unnatural extension of life. She refused to suppress her hatred for this reclusive multi-billionaire, often making profane jokes at his expense. But Morgan wanted the most gifted experts on the planet. He knew they would work tirelessly to keep him alive. Always the consummate professional, she barks out the obvious rundown.

"Heartbeat is irregular. Pressure is dropping."

"He's fading fast." Doctor Douglas chimes in.

A sandy-haired, thirty-something heart specialist who, ironically, has such a mean streak that he's already on Beta-blockers. Life has been kicking him in the gonads for years now, and he carries the extreme anger issues to prove it. He watches the blinking on the monitor slow to a crawl, trying to hide the cruel grin curling his lips. The irregular beeps of someone barely hanging on suddenly stop dead. The room fills with a monotonous drone, signaling it's time to call the undertaker.

"Some funeral director should have that flatlining sound as his ringtone." Douglas jokes.

26

"Cardiac arrest. 10 cc's of adrenaline, stat." Ericson orders.

Having anticipated what was going to happen, Sheila slaps the already-prepared needle into the physician's hand. He wastes no time administering the drug. The entire crew ceases their activities and goes silent. They huddle over the patient like they're watching a football game, hoping the brave young quarterback launches a Hail Mary pass and somehow sends it into overtime. But their heroics fail: the injection barely causes a blip on the screen. Sheila rolls the defibrillator up to the bed and rips out the electrode paddles.

She squirts the conducting gel onto one side, vigorously rubs them together, and hands them to the doctor.

"Clear."

He shocks the patient's chest, causing the decrepit body to convulse like an ancient mummy coming back to life after centuries of living death. The heart monitor continues to hum its dreaded tune.

"Increase the voltage. Give it the maximum."

Douglas spins the voltage dial-up like it were a volume control and his favorite jam just came on the car radio. The doctor smears the paddles together once again, then hits his patient hard. As if he is trying to transmit his own adrenaline into the old guy's heart and get it pumping again.

"Live. Live, damn you," he says.

"Nothing. No change." the nurse reports, stating the obvious. The doctor stares down in frustration at his patient's lifeless face, ripping off his gloves in anger. This act brings a soothing, liberated expression to his face. He's free. Instead of whipping them to the floor as he intended, he sighs and places them gently on the bed in reverence.

"Okay, that's it. We've known it was coming since we were hired. I'm calling it at..." he glances at his watch "6:48. Cause of death... complications from pancreatic cancer."

The room is filled with murmurs. A few of the members are dejected, but most are derisively happy. Sheila takes nasty joy in switching off the heart monitor, smashing that switch as if she were snapping the patient's neck.

"So, this is how it ends for Jackson Morgan." the doctor interjects. "I don't think many people will feel sorry for him."

"Sorry? For him?" Douglas asks.

"You've got to be kidding," Sheila adds.

"Look at that ring. It's worth more than I'd make in ten lifetimes."

They gaze at the stunning ring fossilized into the tycoon's finger, his infamous trademark. A massive, priceless emerald, surrounded by diamonds, pronged onto a platinum band. He had "acquired" it in a ruthless legal battle with a Middle Eastern prince over a legal settlement. The emir reportedly had his most revered cleric place a curse upon it before handing it over. Morgan worshipped it more zealously than the proudest parents on earth treasured their children. He never removed it from his hand.

"This bastard embezzled billions of dollars from the retirement funds of millions of decent, hard-working Americans," Douglas says.

"And while he squandered their money on yachts and mansions and World-Class whores, those people lost their jobs, their homes, everything," Sheila adds.

Douglas rips electrodes and intravenous connectors off his barely deceased corpse like an Old West dentist yanking teeth out of an outlaw's mouth. Sheila callously tears the plugs from the machinery out of the electrical outlets. Neither display even a hint of remorse for their patient.

Instead, they alternate crude yet honest insults while other personnel packs the implements away.

"My parents invested well during their careers and paid for all my medical school bills." Douglas discloses. "Then this bastard ripped off their entire portfolio. Now we live together in a rat trap apartment in the city because that's all we can afford."

"And the courts let him get away with it," Sheila adds. "He only received six months in a minimum-security tennis resort."

One by one, the other medical crew members nod in disdainful agreement as they evacuate the premises.

"Monster."

"Greedy pig."

"Bastard."

Douglas continues the postmortem celebrity roast continues unabated.

"And after all that, he had the unmitigated balls to appear on one of those televangelists shows, claiming he had seen the light and repented his sins."

"And there are a lot of morons out there who he ripped off that actually believe him, and pray with him on TV, while all that money he stole from them is swimming in interest in a nice, warm Cayman Islands bank account," Sheila says.

Ericson shakes his head with a scowl.

"I guess nowadays all you have to do is pay off the right people and act sorry, and you can get away with anything," he says.

"I truly hate to say this, but Jackson Morgan deserved a far more horrible death," Sheila says.

"If he wasn't on Death's Door already, I was tempted to sneak in one night and pull the plug myself," Douglas admits.

Morgan's cadaver begins stirring, barely noticeable to the naked eye. As if this derogatory ranting about him has enraged his spirit. It twitches strangely. The fluorescent lights flicker simultaneously. The machines still plugged in pulsate on and off, as if the electrical current they were connected to is wavering. Weird shadows glide eerily around the corners of the room. A ghostly shape rises ominously from the corpse, invisible to the busy staff members. It is the soul of the recently deceased, hovering like an angry storm cloud over his own withered frame. He slowly reawakens in this ethereal state. His consciousness melds into its new invisible existence, behaving as egotistically in death as he was in life.

"What do you mean I deserved a horrible death? I'll have you checking for STDs in a prison hospital for the rest of your insignificant life, you peasant. I'll... wait... what?"

Morgan's face turns a whiter shade of pale as he realizes he is somehow suspended in midair. He swims his limbs around like an astronaut in zero gravity yet can't come to grips with his newly acquired form. The twitching now becomes frantic trembling, his tone hastily retreats to an uneasy tirade.

"What kind of hospital is this? Do you always hang your patients from the ceilings? Get me down from here."

The medical team goes about their business, oblivious to Morgan's otherworldly plight. His jowls tense up, his dentures gnash almost audibly. This old tycoon is accustomed to having his every whim immediately attended to by whatever poor serf had the misfortune to be waiting on him. But the med team continues to joke about as they work, ignoring his bizarre apparition levitating above their heads. And his uncontrollable weightlessness is exacerbating this already frightening experience.

"This is unacceptable. Where are my lawyers? Nothing will bring me more joy than suing this hospital into bankruptcy."

While he raves on, his intimidating tone is now tinged with dread. The transformation from a disease-ridden geriatric to floating around like a "Get Well" balloon has left him confused. And letting his anger always dominate his emotions is preventing him from realizing what he has become.

Just then, the doors are shoved open from the outside. Two men dressed in emerald-green smocks stride into the room with the swagger of a pair of CIA hitmen. One towers over everybody else like an escapee from the World Wrestling Federation. He wears a name tag that says "Rock". The other, not as huge though just as intimidating, has a badge saying "Diesel". The pair shove through the regular staff members straight to Morgan's bed.

"We'll take it from here." Rock declares.

"Who are these two?" Morgan whines from his paranormal plane of existence.

Ericson strides up, posturing for a confrontation.

"What's going on? Morgan put me in charge here. This isn't standard hospital procedure."

"Back off, scrubs." Diesel blurts out. "We have all the proper authority."

He flashes a medical form in the doctor's face just long enough to prove that he didn't care about procedure. They flex their muscles and flash menacing sneers, which are threatening enough to scare away the entire crew. This unknown duo is in charge now. Most of the team happily walk off for a much-needed break. The ghost of Jackson Morgan drifts above the situation helplessly. The men snatch up his carcass and unceremoniously dump him onto a gurney the way a butcher tosses a quarter cow. Morgan cries out as he recognizes his own mournful face below.

"Wait. Is that me? I demand to know what the hell is going on around here."

He shakes his bony fist at them in a lame attempt to attract attention. He notices to his horror that it was completely transparent, even his famous ring. Rock and Diesel pull the sheet up over his face. The universal rite of passage from life into whatever comes after.

"This is not right. This can't be happening."

The still seething Ericson barges in front of the doorway, trying to impede their progress.

"Hey, you guys can't..."

"We have an order to pick up one body. Don't make me change it to two." Rock says. Ericson droops his posture and reluctantly steps aside. The thuggish pair shove the billionaire's barely deceased cadaver out the door to meet an uncertain destiny.

"Rich or poor, they all end up the same." Rock smirks.

"Yeah, worm food." Diesel cackles as they rumble down the corridor. Morgan makes a pathetic attempt at paddling his astral image out the door but finds himself powerless to stop them.

"Wait. Where are you going? Bring that back. Bring me back here immediately." But it's no use. He peers outside the threshold just in time to see them roll his carcass into the elevator.

The pair chuckle morbidly as the doors ring shut. His body is gone. Now he is panic-stricken and petulantly turns back to the doctor in distress.

"Doctor, you've got to help me. Please. Where are they taking me?" Ericson is blind and deaf to the spectral businessman.

"Well, I guess he's off to the morgue, or wherever."

"That was too freaky." Sheila chimes in.

"I've never seen anything close to that ever happening in this hospital."

"Or any hospital," Douglas adds.

"Where do you think they're taking him?"

"I guess that they were hired by Morgan to take charge of his remains after he passed away so that nobody desecrated his corpse. There are millions of folks out there who would love to get a chance to tear him a new one."

"They'll probably perform an autopsy to verify the cause of death." the nurse speculates. Morgan's eyes widen with fear at the mere mention of the word.

"Autopsy? No. You can't let them dissect me like some biology class frog. I'm still here. I'm just having one of those near-death experiences." Morgan cries as the medical staff starts to turn off the machines.

"Bring my body back. I'm not ready to go. I paid you ungodly sums of money to keep me alive. Use this expensive equipment and revive me. Bring me back," Morgan weeps as the last attendants walk out the door. They switch off the lights behind them, leaving his levitating ghost alone and destitute.

"Please... please... help... me..." he laments. He is alone in the darkness for the longest time. Or maybe it is just an instant. Suddenly, the bitter rage that drove him to become the depraved monster he was burst back out of nowhere to envelop the room.

"NO. You can't do this to me. I'm Jackson Morgan. I elect Presidents. I order wars to start. You peons have no jurisdiction over my soul. I'll have your jobs for this. I'll turn this hospital into a slave labor camp. I will Holocaust all your asses."

His threats are greeted only with mocking echoes, followed by a hollow silence. He hovers aimlessly, existing simultaneously as a bitter old man and a panic-stricken toddler. Angry and helpless. What can a mortal do when they are utterly lost, with no idea of how to return from desolation? Or any idea of how to cope with this anti-reality? Without warning, a bright light appears above him. An indescribable luminescence that draws him towards it with a magnetic grace.

"What is that? Is that what I think it is? No, I don't want to... go. It's not my time yet. But it's so... beautiful."

This was no ordinary ceiling fixture bulb. Not even the Sun in all its magnificence could match this intensity. It grew bigger and brighter with each passing moment. Morgan is awestruck by its warmth and transcendence. Colors begin to swirl around inside, a palette even Van Gogh would be jealous of. Some shades that don't even exist in the mortal plane. He is mesmerized. His mouth drops open as if the jawbone has slipped out of its socket.

The light shoots up through the ceiling, stretching the psychedelic whirlpool out to form an endless tunnel into infinity. Though a part of him still wanted to remain, he was like a moth drawn to a flame. Unconcerned with his safety, as long as he could be one with the brilliant blaze.

He drifts slowly upwards through the otherworldly channel. Gorgeous tints and hues flash past as he accelerates. The tunnel bends and shifts through time and space, as he whirls up and around at dizzying speeds. His mortal frailties are washed away as he travels, cleansing his spirit with heavenly precision. Most of his corrupt earthly desires are left behind. An unquenchable yearning to become one with the Universe blossoms throughout his being

Just before he became one with Infinity, an angelic figure appears before him in the center of the light. The most hauntingly exquisite creature imaginable. Morgan's ethereal journey came to a screeching halt before the divine entity. He had so many fears of what he would encounter when he passed away. Kept them locked away as a prisoner in a secret corner in the back of his mind. But now they returned with a vengeance to terrorize him.

The Angel glows unbearably bright, yet that is not the reason he could not bear to face it. He cowers his eyes because of shame. As memories of the atrocities he had committed on innocent people flood his mind, wispy visions of dozens of sad people emerge. They wander around in the background, multiplying into hundreds, then thousands, murmuring mournfully.

He soon recognizes that they are the phantoms of his countless victims, righteously pointing at the billionaire with otherworldly animosity.

Morgan is paralyzed with dread. His mental capacity shrinks to that of a child. The Angel lords over him, dominating his very essence. He bristles with the thoughts of what eternity had in store for him. And then his trial begins.

"Speak." the Angel proclaims with a deafeningly exalted voice. He simply whimpers, in such shock that his mind finds it impossible to even form a rational thought, let alone words.

"Speak I say." the thunderous voice repeats.

Morgan takes a long pause to calculate what he wanted to say, then finds the courage to speak up.

"Who... who are you? Where am I? I want to know what's happening,"

The angel sweeps up its wings majestically, growing vastly larger and intimidating than he was just seconds before. The mogul is taken aback and gulps back his impudence.

"You know where you are." the angel intones.

"You have secretly dreaded this moment for your entire adult life. It is time for your Final Judgement."

Morgan had thought he was safely in the light, already on his way to Heaven. Now he knew he is on trial for his eternal life, trembling with the fear of the unforgivable.

"But this isn't fair. I was going to change. I was going to make up for all the..."

"All the horrible atrocities you committed upon your fellow human beings. Is that what you were meaning to make up for?"

"Yes, I was.

You took me too soon. You didn't give me time enough to..."

The angel's face swells molten with anger.

"There isn't enough time in all of Creation to make up for the suffering you caused. Your selfishness made good people turn to evil. Left hard-working people starving in the streets. Made people who loved life more than anything take their own."

"But I really was starting to change. I went on TV with Reverend Green and repented my sins for all the world to see."

"That charlatan? He will be facing his own fate soon, and it won't be pleasant. You spoke the words with the lying tongue of the Deceiver. You made a mockery of all that truly spiritual people hold sacred."

Realizing he has no defense for his incredibly cruel actions, Morgan changes tactics and drops to his knees to grovel woefully at the Angel's feet.

"Just give me another chance. Put me back in my body. I'll make it up to them. I swear."

"You no longer have any rights to your body. What is at stake here is your immortal soul."

Now completely frantic, Morgan attempts to dig his way out of this mess with the heinous skill of a satanic criminal defense attorney.

"Please, there has to be something you can do. I know how I committed many terrible crimes. It wasn't my fault. There were extenuating circumstances." The cross wrinkles on the Angel's face melt away. His wings curl back up with a wisp of smoke, and his persona quells as a parent might to a misbehaving child.

"We know of your childhood, and how you were raised. That could be the reason your actions later in life were so corrupt."

Now feeling as if he finally has a leg to stand on, Morgan responds with the sob story of the millennia.

"What childhood? My father only came into my room to beat the hell out of me. My Mother's only sober words to me were how I ruined her life, or how she'd wished I was never born. I ran away when I was 13. I worked my butt off and deserved everything I owned."

"Or stole." the Angel says, turning vengeful once again. Morgan is about to deny the charge, the way he always had on Earth. But he realizes who he's talking to and remains silent. The Angel's tone softens to a hushed tone, his expression more lenient.

"Many a decent soul has been turned to evil by undeserving parents. So, against my better judgment, it has been decided that you shall receive one last chance."

The swindler can hardly contain himself over this unbelievable stroke of good fortune.

"Oh, thank you so much. You won't regret this. I'll become a much better human being. A saint, you'll see."

"You will have no memory of your past life. If you become a decent man, there may still be hope for you. Farewell for now."

"Wait. No memory? How will I know how to behave? I'll have to try to remember this,"

But the Angel has no interest in being in the tycoon's presence any longer. One wave of his wing and Morgan is crushed back through the tunnel, the weight of the Universe collapsing on his shoulders. As his essence spirals downwards, he feels his entire consciousness being ripped apart. He wails in unimaginable pain as

36

his soul inside putrefies, then reforms into a globule in the pit of his stomach. The roller coaster ride makes him so nauseated; he regurgitates his soul from his mouth. It permeates the colors of the tunnel with the darkness, the foul essence of Jackson Morgan.

He was being dragged at tortuous speeds through his own diseased sins. The stench of his foul misdeeds inflamed his nostrils like he was inhaling napalm.

The screaming of the pain he caused the innocents shattered his eardrums. Their gut-wrenching fingernails, sharp as Satan's talons, shred him the entire way down the shaft, causing excruciating agony that no mortal could even conceptualize. His spirit blistered and melted from the sheer friction as if he was descending into Hell. He was being shown how utterly unbearable Eternity would be if he failed.

And then it was over.

A quaint little room in the maternity ward of Hollis General Hospital is occupied this momentous day by one Chloe Carter. Picking the wrong guy has turned her once-promising life into a sordid soap opera. Instead of flaunting her pouty lips and shaking her scandalous butt at the local clubs, she is mired in the thralls of tortuous childbirth. She sweats and strains alone, forsaken by family and friends because of a few exquisitely stupid recent life choices. Once loved for her academic achievements, she is now ostracized for headlining a few too many police blotters. Cut off from Mom's scrumptious home cooking, she is now a gaunt version of what she once was.

Crusty old Doctor Rock flares his hairy nostrils and exhales his V.S.O.P. breath as he struggles to feign interest in this blessed event. Monday is the worst day to have a medical procedure because many physicians are still hungover from the weekend. He fumbles around as if ninety percent of his brain is on the golf course. One of those guys who would have retired years ago if he could stand staying at home with his wife.

Assisting is nurse Abby Jenkins, a garden gnome of a woman who wears her uniform so tightly it has squeezed every drop of empathy from her soul. Abby flaunts her resting bitch face as a badge of honor. The look of a woman whose cat craps in her shoe every morning. She screams at poor Chloe as if she had just sideswiped her car.

"Push Chloe. Push already, dammit. We haven't got all day here." she shouts. Chloe trembles, exhausted after a dozen excruciating hours of childbirth. Her entire body writhes and quivers as if suffering through an exorcism.

"I can't do it. It hurts so bad. I can't take it anymore." Chloe screams pitifully. She finds as much sympathy as a cut-rate comedian bombing at an open mike night. Rock is a moment away from ordering a c-section. Jenkins has heard it all before and has no respect for unwed mothers and welfare babies.

"You better start pushing harder this instant, or I'll push you out into the parking lot and you can have some homeless bum deliver your little bastard."

Chloe is so naïve and in so much pain that in her drugged-out state of mind, she almost believes the nurse's threat. It scares her into one last desperate effort. All the pain and exasperation finally subside when her newborn child crashes the party at 6:48 in the morning. Doctor Rock nearly drops the slippery infant and shoves it at Jenkins like an unwelcome bag full of dog poop. The cord is cut, the baby is wiped clean, and the nurse hands it over to the new mother wiggling like a newly caught trophy bass at the nearby fishing hole.

"It's a boy." the doctor says, as happy to be done with the birth as Chloe.

"Seems healthy enough. Won't stop crying, though."

Chloe clutches her little rascal with all the tenderness she can muster. She's just suffered through half a day of labor that few men could endure. But even in his mother's care, the obstinate baby won't stop wailing. He stares up at his mother with the gaze of someone who knows his existence is about to be terminated. Out of nowhere, a sparkling shaft of nearly invisible colors shoots down through the ceiling like a laser beam, striking the infant dead center on the forehead. He winces and squirms when it hits, then tranquilizes, seeming to be somehow absorbing the cosmic rays.

"What was that?" Chloe cries out.

"What was what?" Jenkins asks. She and Doctor Jones are both completely oblivious to the otherworldly event. They both glance around the room, thinking she had spotted a mouse scampering across the floor. Or a cockroach crawling up the wall.

"I just saw some sort of lights. It was like a kaleidoscope. It went right into the baby. Like a rainbow." The disgruntled pair of medical professionals roll their eyes at each other as if an old married couple irritated by their daughters' flights of fancy.

"Chloe, you've been given a lot of medication," Rock says gruffly. "It was just a trick of the eyes."

Chloe can see the exasperation in their eyes and timidly acquiesces.

"Okay. I guess you're probably right." Chloe replies with a hint of doubt. "Sure was weird, though."

They attempt to forget it. Yet the trio notices something peculiar. Right after Chloe saw the light enter the baby, the incessant crying had spontaneously ceased. He was resting in her arms, calm and peaceful as a wise old sage. Even the skeptical Jenkins is puzzled.

Whatever strange thoughts were buzzing around their minds vanished when there is a tentative knock at the door. The scraggly visage of Brock Kelly strolls in, wearing enough tattoos and piercings to make any would-be father-in-law consider hiring a hitman. "B-Rock" is a part-time bass player in a sleazy punk rock band. He's also a part-time drug dealer, part-time armed robber, and part-time human being, living his barely marginal life like a mental patient with multiple personalities.

For this, the birth of his first (?) child, he decides to show up bearing gas station flowers and a creepy but sincere smile. He appears genuinely happy that his offspring has apparently been born normal and did not spew forth already adorned with meth-teeth and track marks.

"Hi, baby. Can I come in?" he asks.

"Of course, Brock, come in and see your son. He's such a little sweetheart."

He lurches in nervously, as if afraid to be here. Takes a seat at the edge of the bed, gazing at the little tyke in awe. He touches him gently and jibber jabbers a little baby talk. The newborn completely ignores him.

"If it's alright with you, I've decided to name him Jack." Chloe declares.

"Okay with me. Hiya Jack. How'd you come up with that one? We've been thinking for months, and you hated every name we came up with."

Chloe stares at him for a moment, her mind blanking out. She glances up to the ceiling as if looking for an answer. Nothing registers.

"I have no idea. It just came to me."

They stare into each other's eyes; the way couples do when they haven't seen each other for months. Both look semi-ashamed and turn away out of deep-seated embarrassment.

"How ya feeling, girl? You look pretty ragged, all I'm sayin'" Brock blurts out.

Chloe overlooks the rude comment and takes the conversation in another direction, like a tennis player backhanding a volley.

"We can't live the way we did before, Brock." She whispers in his ear. "Not with a baby. Robbing liquor stores is no way to provide for a family."

"I know, I know." Brock retorts, throwing up his hands in frustration to avoid the subject. "But ya know you were almost as guilty as I was."

Chloe keeps silent till Rock and Jenkins take the hint and vacate the premises.

"You nearly killed that cop," she whispers with pangs of regret.

"The bullet didn't even hit him."

40

"But you were aiming, I know you were. You were just too wasted to hit anything."

Brock's temper flares but seeing the baby in her arms stops him from arguing anymore and digging himself into an even deeper hole.

"You're right. You're right. We hafta change." he agrees, then quickly changes the subject. "Hey, little guy. We're gonna have a great life together, the three of us."

Chloe rewards him with a sad emoji smile, happy at least says he wants to change. She longs to tell him so many things. What her dreams are. What she wants her life to be. How she wants him to be around a lot more, not hanging with his loser friends. And not because he had to, but because he wanted to be there. For her and the baby. Why can't guys read minds, so that girls didn't have to keep explaining their desires in life to them? Over and over again. Especially since many times, they changed from day to day, even moment to moment.

So frustrating.

But her needs would have to wait for another time. A smarmy police officer with 12 pack abs and a snarl on his lips enters the room. They both know why he's there.

"Please, can't I stay a few more minutes?" Brock pleads. "I hardly had any time…"

The cop cuts him off like he was speeding through traffic for Dunkin Donuts.

"Yeah, yeah, yeah… too bad. The labor took too long," he says with a savage grin. "You're going back to your happy little cell. Your butt buddies can't wait for you to get home."

For no reason other than to be cruel, he unleashes his hostility on Chloe.

"Next time, spit out your bastards quicker, bitch. C'mon, tough guy, turn around."

The cop taunts the new dad, waving a pair of handcuffs in front of his eyes. B-rock reluctantly does an about-face, and the bracelets are squashed onto his wrists like two tourniquets meant to cut off the blood supply. The prisoner winces but holds in the pain silently to himself.

"Take care of the baby, hon." he uncomfortably squeaks out. "With good behavior, I should be out in ten months."

He leans over to kiss her and the baby goodbye, then bites his lip till it almost bleeds. The terrible conditions in state prisons are no secret. There is a strong possibility this could be the last time he would see either one of them.

"Be careful. I love you." she cries.

"Yeah, yeah, yeah, enough with the drama." the cop interrupts. "You're making me cramp up from my breakfast burrito. Get moving, pillow biter, before I shove my nightstick up your ass."

The cop kidney prods the helpless Brock out of the room, Chloe sighs back into the soiled bedding, frightened and abandoned. Her eyes pool up, grieving for Brock and herself. She has so many critical questions yet knew this toddler masquerading as a man had none of the answers. She would be saddled with all the physical and financial responsibilities of raising their child for the foreseeable future. That thought slammed her in the face just as the door slammed behind them.

Tears shower down like a cloudburst that was long overdue. She hugs her baby tighter, hoping to receive some type of hope and reassurance from this tiny being she had just given birth to. Instead, he lets out a demonic growl and shoves her away, struggling to get away from her. Chloe feels such an emptiness inside as if her soul had sweat out of her body into the mattress. As if giving life to Jack had ended her own.

It's a beautifully sunny day in the city park. Hot enough to make a person happy to be alive, yet not stifled and sweaty.

Squirrels scamper around foraging for food. Pigeons meander about, cooing softly. That is until Chloe and her now five-year-old son Jack pedal their bikes up the asphalt pathway. The squirrels suddenly scamper up the trees for cover. The pigeons squabble, nervously bobbing their heads and crapping up the sidewalks.

They ride over to meet Chloe's friend as she perches on a bench. Kelly is a preppie princess, dressed as upscale as possible without being gauche. She pays a watchful eye to her son Nick, a waddling toddler with a Kool-Aid smile and all the charm of a slightly soiled diaper. He squats in a sandbox 20 feet away, playing with his toys. Kelly looks happy to see Chloe but gives her son a McKayla sneer. She doesn't even say "Hello", simply rattles off a Parental Disclaimer.

"Chloe, are you sure your son will behave this time?"

Chloe stands her bike off to the side with the kickstand and approaches her overtly blunt friend. Moms have a somewhat war-torn appearance from the everyday rigors of rearing kids, but Chloe looked like she'd been tortured at Guantanamo Bay.

Rather than a few happy wrinkles of sleeplessness, she bore the deep, grim lines of sheer exhaustion and despair.

"He'll be fine, won't you, Jack?" Chloe states in a less-than-convincing voice. But her son completely ignores her. He tosses his training wheel cycle to the pavement like it's stolen and races for the sandbox with a backpack full of toys.

Nick twitches nervously, frightened of the intrusive newcomer. Jack long jumps into the sand like an Olympic athlete. He lands full force, spraying a load of granules right into Nick's face. The poor kid has to squint and cough, then clumsily tries to brush it away like he's been hit with a pie. Jack lets out a cruel laugh at his awkward predicament. He pours his impressive collection of brand-new trucks and action figures out onto the play area. Nick's eyes widen at the sight of such amazing playthings and naively accepts that this unfamiliar playmate is safe and Mommy-Approved.

"Kelly, I am so happy you met up with me today. People are so distant lately. Brock and I have…"

"It's not you two, Chloe.' Kelly interrupts, eyes rolling with moral superiority. "Everyone thinks that you've done an amazing job turning your lives around. Frankly, the problem is your son."

Kelly consciously glares towards Jack, who playfully zooms his toy spaceship as high as he could stretch into the blue sky. When

Kelly turns away, he crashes it into a group of unwary action figures, screaming out their death throes with sadistic glee. Although he owns every toy he ever whined for, Jack jealously eyes one of Nickie's favorite Hot Wheels.

"I know Jack gets a little aggressive sometimes, but his counselor at school says it's just a phase and he'll grow out of it," Chloe protests. Meanwhile, her son snatches away the prized vehicle. When Nick wobbles up to his feet to protest, Jack gives him a cruel shove back down onto the hard wooden railroad tie which surrounds the sandbox.

"I hope so because the other mothers and I are deeply concerned for the safety of our children. It's as if your boy was born evil." Kelly rants as Nick bravely rises to try to get his beloved Hot Wheel back. But Jack sucker-punches him, knocking him back to the earth, wailing in tears. Both women rush over to see what happened.

"Mommy, he stole my car, and then he hit me. Hard in the face." Nick proclaims.

Kelly whirls around, laser beam eyes searing into Chloe.

"This is how you teach him to behave? Not even 5 minutes and your bastard has already injured my baby."

"I'm sure it was an accident. Jack, you didn't hit him, did you?"

"Nope," Jack answers nonchalantly.

"He hit him. You know he did." Kelly concludes while gathering up her son's toys.

"The other mothers were right. I tried to give you one last chance because I really care for you. But don't ever call me again. Your son is a menace. He needs to be institutionalized."

Kelly stuffs the menagerie into her stroller and picks up the still bawling Nick. She storms off across the winding lane, his whimpering fading away as they distance themselves from Chloe and Jack forever. Chloe looks destitute, watching her last friend in the world disappearing like a sad memory. She turns to her son with a final gasp of blind faith.

"You didn't hurt him on purpose, did you?"

Jack admits to nothing and simply goes on playing with his toys as if nothing ever happened. Although the nasty partial smile on the opposite side of his face tells a different story. Chloe sinks to her knees on the beach-like sand, tears welling in her eyes. The sobbing flows out in rhythmic waves as Kelly sails out of sight. She realizes whatever hope she had for any type of friendship was gone as long as her spawn is around. She has been given a life sentence to the bitter, desolate prison that Jack had relegated her to.

Thirteen lonely years have passed. Jack is now eighteen, laying on the bed in his room with his head propped up by extra pillows. His once puffy cheeks have thinned into angular cheekbones, the once chubby little toddler has evolved into a wiry yet impressive physique.

His eyes show an intense understanding of life and all it has to offer. Not the drive to better himself, but to make himself feel he's better than anyone else. Genetics have awarded him the necessary attributes to be a star athlete or class valedictorian in high school. But a long list of suspensions and expulsions prove that he will never head anyone's Dean's List.

He's browsing the web while also intermittently texting his friends at the same time as most kids do these days. But he's not YouTubing the hottest new music or asking where the next big party is being thrown. He is searching for luxury items of the rich and famous and several not-very-legal ways to obtain them. His taste in toys has matured. The boy who was once so interested in Hot Wheels is now obsessed with the actual vehicles themselves. And devious ways to make enough money to obtain them.

Drastic schemes to procure wealth with minimum chances of getting caught. How to have lots of fingers in other people's pies. And snatch them away when the real owners aren't paying attention.

Suddenly, Chloe bursts into his room. The years have not been as kind to her as they have to Jack. She is as haggard as a woman twice her age should be. A face can show wrinkles that grew from smiling. And deep furrows that grew from sadness. But hers were tortuous creases from a life of relentless desperation. Her hair have withered, her jowls have sagged, and if you caught her in the right light, her skin has a slightly yellowish discoloration from long, sordid misadventures with cheap tequila. She is in near hysterics, ready to explode with unbearable news.

"Jack. Tiffany is in the hospital. They say she tried to commit suicide."

"Yeah, I know," Jack mutters matter-of-factly.

His mother is stunned by his heartless response.

"You knew? Why didn't you tell me? Why aren't you there taking care of her?" she shouts. "You've been dating for over two years. You're basically engaged." But she spots that narcissistic look in his eyes and knows that once again, her son had bitterly disappointed her. "So, this was just an act? All the romance and plans for a future with Tiffany were just one big charade?"

Jack stays mute as is his custom. A silent man will never be caught in a lie. He attempts to change the subject, waving an envelope up to her reddening face.

"Look, I've been admitted to Princeton. Full scholarship." Chloe rips the letter away and tears it into a dozen pieces, which drift slowly to the ground like forgotten dreams.

"Oh my God. Your father was right. No wonder he left us years ago. They were right. All these years defending you, but now it's finally so crystal clear. You are evil."

"I'm not evil. Mass murderers and child molesters are evil. I'm being practical, Mother."

"You practically are a child molester. You're 18, Tiffany is barely 16. You told her you loved her."

"I do love her. I love how she looks. I love how she feels. I love things she does for me."

"You bastard." Chloe slaps him hard, again and again. Not like an angry mother. The way a Holocaust survivor would slap her Nazi jailer if she had the chance. Jack found his breaking point. He grabs her wrist and twists it painfully to pull himself up out of bed. Rather than showing mercy to the woman who gave him life, he slaps her

46

right back. He forces her face eye to eye with his, snarling like a rabid dog.

"You emotional fool. I won't let love, pity, or guilt drag me down. No preppie nympho from the shallow end of the gene pool is going to interfere with my life plans."

He releases her with an angry shove, then calmly sits at his desk in front of his laptop. Chloe stands there, whimpering, trembling. Not only from the slap, but from the thought of the wasted years she spent nurturing this vile creature.

"I heard rumors about you on the phone. People have been saying things, things I refused to believe."

"What were they saying, Mother?" Jack replies with an irritated groan.

"They say the reason Tiffany tried to commit suicide is that she's pregnant. That you told her if she tried to prove the baby was yours, you would make her life unbearable." She limps morosely towards the doorway. "I told myself it couldn't be true; my son could never do that. Because if it was true, then the last 18 years of my life have been a pathetic waste. But it is true, isn't it?"

Jack switches back into airplane mode, smiling heartlessly as he turns back to his laptop screen, as silent as a blind date's phone.

"Go to Princeton or go to Hell. Just be out of my house by tomorrow. And never show your face at my door again."

Chloe is ready to slam his door shut in anger but refuses to give him the satisfaction. She will not waste another ounce of energy on Jack again. She wanders away lost and dazed like a beaten puppy whose owners abandoned her in the street. Jack chuckles to himself, so warped that he is actually amused by the whole horrible melodrama he had created.

The sun blazes above in the midday sky while waves crash below a treacherous cliff along the California coast. A brand-new serpent green Ferrari convertible speeds up a slender canyon road behind a white Prius, like a hungry snake chasing a poor little pet mouse. It squeals into the passing lane to overtake the hapless vehicle. Just then, a Hummer limousine bears down in the opposite direction. The

Ferrari swerves back into traffic, just before both cars crash over the side of the mountain.

Jack is the driver, four years older and ten times more insidious. His psychotic laugh drowns out the engine as he escapes a fiery death by mere inches. His stunning new wife Cara also laughs but with a hint of anxiety. Perhaps because she narrowly avoided wetting her pink designer skirt that barely covered her privates.

"Jack, you're a psycho," she screams over the throaty rumble of the engine. The wind blows back her naturally auburn hair, revealing the gorgeous face of a princess. Flawless velvety skin, killer bod, and eyes the exact emerald shade as the car they were breaking the speed limit in. She is a bit of a pampered brat but gifted with the old soul of a chronic optimist. And for whatever reason, she is head over 6-inch pumps crazy in love with Jack.

"You still love me, though," he shouts, his insatiable ego thirsting for any drop of worship he can conjure up. He had blazed his way through Princeton, regarded as a shooting star of intellect. But in reality, he was just a dirty snowball with a rock inside, viciously cold and potentially deadly. He received impeccable accolades in academics through his devious expertise in three key subjects that were never taught there: bribery, blackmail, and extortion. With these vile skills, he had worked his way into the fraternity of most ultra-elite students. Slithered into the secret societies that would otherwise be off-limits to undergrads with his socially and financially laughable status. He used hired thugs to coerce the Ivy League's most honored faculty members into giving him straight A's while rarely attending class, let alone completing assignments.

He built up brownie points by doing questionable favors for the offspring of the rich and famous. Obtaining the best illegal substances. Providing the finest in female companionship. Having rivals and undesirables violently assaulted. So many of the aristocratic college boys he encountered owed him favors. He could launch a start-up business today and have it immediately listed as a hot buy on the Nasdaq tomorrow. And he used his repellant ethics to lure poor undergrad Cara into a relationship. She fell for his dirty tricks like daddy's personal safe plummeting off an ivory tower.

"Are you happy, sweetheart?" she asks.

"Of course," Jack replies with all the honesty of a serial killer taking a polygraph. He taps the brakes as they approach green, ivy-covered gates that signal the end of the road. They reminded him of the entrance to the old "Falcon Crest" estate, an old television show that his babysitter once tried to force him to watch.

Tried. She never "tried" that again.

"Here we are...Home Sweet Home."

Jack slinks his car up the drive and stops, reaching out to press the intercom button. A dignified voice promptly answers.

"Harlow residence. Whom may I ask is calling?"

"Dawson. It's me, Cara," she says, honestly elated to hear her family butler's articulate tone once again.

"Oh, Miss Harlow. So wonderful to have you home again. I'll buzz you in"

The heavenly gates sweep back, revealing the spectacle of wealth that is the Harlow Estate. First, he is greeted by wondrous gardens, exquisite marble statues, and a fountain that must have been imported from a town in France. The serpentine lane leads up to the main mansion, a massively breathtaking combination of art and architecture. Cara's tedious descriptions of her childhood home could never have prepared Jack for this overwhelming display.

"Isn't it dreamy?" she fawns with a sentimental sigh.

"Jackpot," Jack whispers to himself in reply. His eyes narrow and his mouth salivates. He resembles an evil Leprechaun who has finally reached the Pot of Gold at the end of some demented rainbow. He snails his vehicle along, soaking in every little nuance of the property he intends to 'inherit' one day. Sooner than later. Parking between the dignified ivory pillars on the front steps, he is impressed to see three valets rush over to open their doors and assist with luggage.

Cara races around the car and snatches up Jack's hand, overeager to be his tour guide to the grandeur of her magnificent manor.

49

She leads him to the ogre-sized front doors, which glide open with a soft hiss without even ringing the bell.

The pair are greeted with the dignified visage of Dawson, a fastidious but compassionate middle-aged man, standing so far upright, he appeared as if he would teeter over backward.

"Miss Harlow, what a joy it is to see you again. You are looking even more vibrant than ever."

Cara leaps at Dawson and squeezes him like an old teddy bear.

"Hello Dawson, you old sweetheart. I missed you so much. This is Jack, my first and only hubby."

Dawson holds out his hand to greet him, but Jack passes him by without even acknowledging his existence. He just stares around in awe, guesstimating at the value of the wealth gathered in this one room alone.

Remarkably, the interior was even more wondrous than the exterior. An expansive foyer leading up to a Gothic arched ceiling that glows with a lustrous sheen. Paintings by Old Masters that would rival any of the world's top art museums line the walls, side by side with eclectic modern art.

"Your father awaits you in his study."

Dawson declares, visibly miffed by Jack's snubbery.

"Thank You, Dawson, Dear. I can't wait for us to have a long heart-to-heart. I want to hear everything that's happening in your life." Cara interjects, clutching his hand. She turns back to Jack, a little peeved herself.

"How could you be so mean to Dawson?"

"What? Oh, whatever, I'm simply in shock at how incredible this place is. You said you grew up in a mansion. But this is more like the palace at Versailles." Jack says.

"Oh, these are just things that our family has collected over the years. They're not as important as being gracious to my friends. And Dawson always cared for me while I was growing up."

"Sorry, Honey, I guess I was just in shock." he poses as a justifiable excuse.

"Well, alright, I forgive you for being so astounded by our beautiful home. But you better be nice to Dad or else I will get this thing annulled so fast." she giggles in jest. They walk arm in arm through hallowed halls so elegant Jack feels as if he's about to meet The Queen of England.

Cara ushers him into a right turn, and they enter the great man's study. Massive bookshelves filled with first editions, along with dozens of glass cases filled with many of the rarest collectibles on the planet. Ancient relics from bygone eras, like Faberge Eggs and Jade Figurines from the Ming Dynasty, sharing the same space as old baseball cards and pristine comic books.

Out of the shadows in a dark corner of the room strides Wilson Harlow, present torchbearer of the family fortune. Much younger looking than his 55 years. He looks as fit and healthy as a man Jack's age. A few wrinkles and gray hairs make him look even more distinguished. Jack is taken aback by the foreboding glare he receives. Harlow's expression makes it abundantly clear he is not pleased that his only daughter decided to elope with a total stranger. He tries to come off as menacing as possible without pointing a shotgun like some deranged hillbilly.

"Daddy." Cara shrieks like a teenager at a Justin Beiber concert. She springs at him with a flying kitten hug that so surprises him that all the pent-up anger he was reserving for his new son-in-law melts away.

"Cara, dear, welcome home," Wilson exclaims, thrilled to see his daughter return. She kisses him so many times that she realized it was starting to look weird and pulls away with a sheepish grin.

"Okay, okay. I missed you, too. If you were so anxious to see me, why didn't you invite me to your wedding"

"Oh, Daddy, I explained that. I told Jack the story of how you and Mom flew off on vacation together to Paris. And you proposed to her at the Louvre. He thought it would be so sweet if we went there and got married just like you."

"But you have a lot more to worry about, dear. After all, you're a Harlow. There are procedures and paperwork and invitations and press conferences…"

"That's exactly what we didn't want to go through. Jack said it would be so much more romantic if we just did it. No ice sculptures, no 50-piece orchestras, no TMZ. Just 2 people who fell in love."

"Well, your knight in shining armor may have swept you off your feet, but what about the financial arrangements?"

"I told you, Daddy, I went behind your back to your lawyers, and they set up an iron-clad prenup. And Jack signed it in front of three witnesses from the firm.

If we get divorced, he gets absolutely nothing."

Wilson finally bites the bullet and gives in. His lawyers had already advised him that the marriage contract was indeed foolproof. If in the future, Jack cheated on or mistreated Cara in any way, shape, or form, all he would get was the proverbial boot. Even if he appealed, his lawyers could only advise him that settling for a small, undisclosed sum was his best option. The reluctantly gracious new father-in-law welcomes Jack into his aristocratic clan with a hearty handshake which grows into a hearty embrace.

"Welcome to the family, Son. You're far from the man I would have chosen for my daughter, but any man who signs the phone book-sized prenup my lawyers showed me must truly love her."

"Thank you, Sir…although I think I should be slightly insulted." Jack declares.

The three break out into laughter, cutting the tension like a knife.

"Well, it's such an honor to meet you, Sir. I have admired you for my entire life. Your hostile takeover of the Corodyne Corporation was ingenious."

"I like him, Cara. He knows how to suck up. Would you enjoy a cognac?"

"Of course."

Wilson pours Jack a generous snifter full of the most expensive cognac available, handing it to him with a cautious glance. He's studying the new bridegroom, his mannerisms, and body language. Trying to get a feel for what he is genuinely like under the façade that he's shown his daughter. Everyone hides their true identity from other people in one way or another, and Mr. Harlow is a master at perceiving their many hidden nuances.

Yet Jack seems to be just as proficient at masking away any character flaws. Like a World-Class Poker Champion, he hides his tells and gives no insight into his private schemes.

Except one. Instead of focusing on Cara, Jack is enthralled with the precious antiquities housed in separate cases at strategic points in the room. The love of beautiful artworks and rare collectibles looks very much different from what Jack is exuding. In some people, greed is a permeable thing, and Jack is oozing it out of all his pores. With every new item he peruses, he guzzles more of the strong liquor. Not like a connoisseur, more like a jealous alcoholic.

"I see you enjoy the finer things in life, my boy." Wilson says, "One of the luxuries of being a Harlow is that we're able to acquire a few of the belongings of many of the wealthy men of the past. Let me give you a quick tour."

Harlow points out two gorgeous pieces nearby, checking to see how Jack will react.

"This painting here once belonged to Joseph Kennedy. That sculpture next to it was once in the Rockefeller mansion."

Jack is calculating in his head how much each item is worth. The grin on his face widens moment by moment. Until they arrive at an object which Jack finds particularly fascinating.

"And this ring was once owned by Ja…"

"Jackson Morgan," Jack says. Wilson and Cara are shocked.

"How in the world did you know that, son? That backstabbing fraud died before you were born."

For once, Jack has no answer, looking quite puzzled himself.

53

"I... I don't know. I must have read about it in a magazine or a biography."

"This was Morgan's most prized possession. He obtained it when he made his first billion. He never took it off. It was pried off his cold, dead hand by the Federal Courts after they decided he had committed so many financial crimes that all of his assets had to be forfeited."

"What? How dare they." Jack cried out as if this decades-old court case involved him personally.

Both Cara and her father are staggered and disconcerted by his bizarre response. The startled looks on their faces shock him out of his temporary fit of madness. He composes himself and pats his hand on Harlow's back. Attempting to smooth over the feathers he most certainly ruffled.

"Whoa, I have no idea where that behavior came from. Sorry."

"Perhaps you should take it easy on the brandy, my boy," Wilson advises.

"Yes, that's probably it," Jack mumbles, setting the glass on a priceless Victorian desk. Cara rushes over and picks it up before it left an indelible circle. Her new love is oblivious, still mesmerized by the ring in the case.

"It's more beautiful than I imagined. Can you remove it from the glass so I could examine it closer?"

"Whatever for?" Wilson asks with a groan.

"I can't say exactly. Something about the ring just reaches out to me. I've never felt anything like this before. It's almost a mystical connection."

Harlow's brow furrows. He was expecting that his daughter's new husband would have a few quirks he found objectionable. Like a love of skateboarding or slouching with his elbows on the dinner table. But this was no quirk. This was a diagnosable abnormality. Cara notices the growing animosity on her beloved father's face and intervenes.

"Please, Daddy. It clearly means a lot to him." Wilson's face softens over his baby's concerns.

"Well, I suppose there's no harm. You being part of the family now."

Wilson touches a circle on the wainscoting that looks like part of an engraved pattern, which opens a hidden sliding door.

He punches in a secret code which turns off the alarm and gently removes the glass case.

"You're going to inherit all this when I'm gone anyway."

He delicately removes the ring from its velvet pillow home and hands it to Jack. Once merely enchanted by the jewelry, the feel of it in the palm of his hand arouses emotions buried in Jack's subconscious. He becomes subjugated, worshipping it as a man possessed. Cara and Wilson are stunned by his strange behavior. An embarrassed Cara tugs at his sleeve, but he ignores her.

"Jack? Jack, what is wrong with you?"

Irritated, Wilson snatches the ring from Jack, who practically snarls back at him in anger. Cara is mortified.

"Easy, Son. I'm not quite dead yet."

Wilson returns the ring to its rightful place in the case with the uneasy stare of someone witnessing a meltdown. Jack's mood brightens as if he was coming out of a trance. He shakes his head, then his entire body, the way a dog spins himself dry when racing into the house after a frightening thunderstorm. He starts to lose his balance and has to recover in one of the museum-piece Early American chairs.

"I'm sorry, sir. I don't know what got into me," Jack mutters, breathing in short bursts like he's having a slight asthma attack. Cara rubs his shoulders, worried sick. This introduction could not be going any worse.

"Really, Dad, he is never like this."

Wilson hovers above with a judgmental expression, perplexed and concerned with his new son-in-law.

55

"Well, Morgan was a nasty bastard. Maybe a little of him rubbed off on you."

Dawson enters the study, interrupting the strange scene.

"Hors d'oeuvres and cocktails are being served in the garden, Sir."

"We're having a small celebration in your honor, honey," Wilson says.

"Wonderful. I think we all need fresh air."

Cara leads the still bewildered Jack outside.

As he wanders off, his eyes still focus on the ring.

The garden party had been expected to be the social event of the season. Instead, it fizzles away like a cheap sparkler. Jack and Cara are saying their goodbyes to the last of the guests. Jack's behavior has destroyed Cara's big night.

"So glad you could come," Cara says. The guests answer with cookie-cutter responses.

"Nice to see you again, dear."

"I hope you and Jack are very happy."

"Have a nice honeymoon."

The crowd wanders back to their vehicles glaring at Jack as if he needed Thorazine and a straitjacket. He stands off to the side like an abandoned mannequin and doesn't even notice.

Dawson closes the garden gate behind them.

"The staff and I will be cleaning up. Will there be anything else, Mr. Harlow?"

"No. I'm going to bed. Goodnight, sweetheart." Wilson says. He gives Cara a kiss, Jack a scowl, and Dawson his empty glass as he storms off to his room.

"Cara, I am so sorry," Jack says.

"Let's just forget it. Hopefully, a good night's sleep will snap you out of whatever funk you're in."

The suite arranged for the couple is as breathtaking as it is massive. Yet in the dark of night, it might just as well be a cell in an affluent asylum. Cara is sleeping, curled up angelically on a bed so enormous you'd need GPS to find your lover. Jack lies wide awake, staring at the ceiling. His vital signs are so hyper; someone would have to shoot him with an elephant tranquilizer to knock him out. Another identity is churning around in his mind, trying to take control.

Finally, he can't take it anymore and erupts out of bed. Ignoring his slippers and robe, he sneaks downstairs into the study and heads straight for the ring. He stares at it like Gollum in The Lord of the Rings, practically drooling, fingers smearing across the glass. Stumbling around in the shadows, he reopens the hidden panel. With the skill of a master safecracker, he has somehow memorized the secret code and switches off the alarm. He slides the glass up and snatches the ring with the frenzy of a man possessed. The mere touch of it on his skin gives him a surge of power.

"What's going on here?"

The lights suddenly flash on. Wilson had been hiding in his corner, waiting to see if he would return. Cara rushes in and they both catch Jack with the ring red-handed.

"Jack, are you insane?"

He ignores her and slips it on. The ring reincarnates the hidden psyche buried in his brain. Jack spins around, throbbing from Morgan's psyche commandeering his body. A surge of memories explodes within him, like binge-watching twenty years of a long-lost tv show in thirty seconds.

"What is this? Can it really be true? It is.

I am Jackson Morgan. I always have been."

Jack suddenly begins to twitch as if from electric shock. Cara screams.

"What's wrong, son?"

"I'm young again. And soon to be richer than ever. I'll kill this old fool off and inherit his wealth and his daughter. I've beaten death. I've beaten death." he screams. Jack laughs maniacally as if he has taken one final gigantic leap off the deep end. He stares at the ring, then at Cara and Wilson, back and forth, laughing harder and harder. Cara screams and curls into her father's arms, covering her face in the folds of his robe. Wilson reaches for the intercom.

"Dawson. Call 911."

Jack's body suddenly freezes still, petrified. The youthful skin on his face mummifies. His eyes drain of color until pure white. He drops to the floor a soulless carcass.

The ring bounces away.

Extraordinary scientific machines play their beeping song in a state-of-the-art medical laboratory. Doctors, nurses, and other technicians huddle around their patient, sitting in a bizarre wheelchair that encases him up to his neck. Tubes connect to IV bags. EKG wires connect to a heart monitoring device. A siren goes off and a warning light begins to blink. The entire team gathers around, murmuring with excitement.

"He's resuscitating."

They all move aside to congratulate each other. As they do, it is revealed that the man in the wheelchair is Jackson Morgan. The billionaire who perished of old age. His body starts to quiver, shaking faster and faster, climaxing in a sudden severe jerk. His entire frame collapses from exhaustion. He soon regains some amount of strength and raises his head with the speed of a sloth. His eyelids creep open, revealing strangely joyful pupils.

"I've beaten Death. I've beaten Death," he mumbles.

Every expression in the room instantly changes to bewilderment. They glance at each other with shocked looks in their eyes.

"How the hell did he know?" the lead doctor wonders.

Morgan, still dazed and groggy, opens and closes his eyes and mouth, seemingly readjusting from one life to another. His consciousness gradually recognizes an unbearable new reality. As if waking up from a nightmare and discovering it wasn't a dream. He tries to reach out to touch one of the doctors, yet his arms refuse to move. Looking down, he finds himself trapped in a futuristic wheelchair, unable to move. A quadriplegic. His terrified eyes plead with the medical team to help him.

"Mr. Morgan. Can you hear me? If you can, please nod your head."

He nods, and the doctor continues as if reporting a miracle.

"Mr. Morgan, you'll be ecstatic when you realize what has happened here."

Tears stream through the wrinkles of his pale, ragged cheeks.

"You are the first human to ever be revived after death. It's incredible, Sir. Exactly what you hoped for when you began financing our project. You'll never have full function of your body, and probably have to live in this wheelchair for the foreseeable future. Still, you've made it back, Sir. You've been reincarnated."

Morgan vision focuses on a sign on the wall that reads "Corodyne Cryogenics"

"Nooooooo!"

Morgan's entire world collapses as he remembers that tragic moment. He had ordered his body to be cryogenically frozen after his death so he could be resuscitated years later when it was medically possible. An ungodly scream bursts from his lips as he grasps the mind-boggling revelation. His soul has just been snatched from the young Jack, soon to be one of the wealthiest 1%, and returned to the pitifully decrepit physique of Jackson Morgan.

"No. Send me back. Send me back."

The doctors glare back and forth at each other, completely puzzled. Why is a man who has just been brought back to life screaming as if he had been sentenced to a living hell?

Outside, a security guard walks over to the door of the cryo room, wondering what the uproar was about. He stares through the small square panel of glass but is unable to see because of the personnel mulling around. He is quickly bored and returns to his seat, surfing his tablet for the top news stories of the day.

"Newlywed Heir To Harlow Fortune Dies Suddenly of Mysterious Disease."

"Soul Purpose"

Ryder Quinn lies in his bed, sleeping peacefully. The one place he can't mess up his life. He has spent his 16 years on this planet hopelessly trapped on the wrong side of the popularity tracks. Definitely not a dweeb, yet nowhere near the hottest guy in 10th grade. Other guys in his grade are taller, yet he's not a toy. Some dudes are way more ripped from lifting weights, yet he's no punk. He's handsome, in an unspectacular way. He has his faults. Slight stuttering, a hint of dorkiness, a tendency to take the lazy way out. And he's screwed up or underachieved so often that it has become ingrained into his mindset. He has unknowingly programmed himself to be less successful in life than he should be.

Or as popular with the ladies. Guys have done a whole lot more with a whole lot less than what he has going for him. He does have a little motivation and self-confidence. But instead of making him appear like a man with a plan, they have the opposite effect. They always seem to get him into trouble. Trouble is his constant companion, his evil, deceased twin brother.

All is dark in his quiet suburban bedroom. He snoozes away, surrounded by posters of the sexiest female celebrities. But they aren't helping his track record. He has nightmares about the embarrassing moves he has attempted on girls that he's been crushing on. Tonight, though, his sleep is peaceful. He drifts through the hours before daylight with the tranquility of a meditating monk.

A sound in the distance grows louder and louder as it gets closer and closer. A 747 jet is approaching, its engines roaring through his open bedroom window, rattling his windowpanes. The noise is so incredibly deafening, any normal kid would be shocked right out of the sack.

But he goes on snoring away, oblivious to the uproar. The plane skies overhead, passes by and heads off to destinations unknown, and Ryder never even notices. He has spent his entire life right near his city's airport. His parent's house lies directly under the flight path of their busiest runway. So, he has grown unconsciously accustomed to the rock concert volume of the aircraft.

His room returns to peaceful serenity. Although not for very long. A faraway reverberation grows to unbearable decibel levels. A freight train is speeding nearer and nearer. The thunderous rumbling of its engines wreaks havoc on the tranquil neighborhood. Outside his vibrating windows, the tracks are merely a hundred feet away. Again, Ryder is utterly unfazed. He slumbers through as if he were born deaf.

His entire room shakes as if a small earthquake is occurring. But he dreams on as if he's on a quiet, empty beach in the middle of nowhere. For whatever reason, the driver hits the brakes. The horrendous screeching of the wheels is so earsplitting it could rip a hole in the space/time continuum. Ryder continues to sleep as if heavily medicated.

Eventually, the train rolls on past, and his run-of-the-mill community is peaceful again. Rip Van Winkle could take lessons from this kid. It appeared as if nothing short of a tornado ripping his house apart would raise him from his coma-like trance. Suddenly, something unnoticeable wakes him with a start. He springs up in bed as if a shotgun blasted off inches from his eardrum.

"What?"

He has not had a dream. Nothing has occurred that should have woken him up so alarmingly. He scans the room, squinting through the moonlight, trying to discern what disturbed him from his slumbers.

"Is someone here?" he asks, a little scared. He can detect a little light snoring from his father in the next room, though it is barely audible. Nothing in the room looks suspicious. He checks his watch, the glow-in-the-dark digital kind. It says "2:11".'

Ryder scratches his head, puzzled that he has no idea what woke him. He's ready to plop his head right back onto his comfy pillows and return to Slumberland. Then an unknown force draws his attention to the open window. A strange sensation of impending danger. The peach fuzz stands up on the nape of his neck. Chills race up and down his spine.

Ryder climbs out of bed more reluctantly than when he has to get up for school. He measures his steps across the minefield of shoes, Legos and video game paraphernalia that obscures the floor. He warily sweeps aside the curtains and investigates his backyard.

It's a long, fenceless stretch of grass leading out to some gravelly railroad tracks.

"Brett? Jason?" he calls out, thinking that two of his friends from school may be out there pulling a prank. But the entire area is deserted as a graveyard. Not a soul is out there. Both neighbors' yards on either side are empty as well. Not even a cricket chirping. Ryder quivers from one of those frightened twitches, still a bit uneasy. He spins around on his bed to get comfy, in need of some serious sack time. A sudden stiff breeze blows the curtains up, and they swipe him in the backside. The weird sensation startles him a little. He runs off to bed, crawls under the covers, and squishes his eyes shut.

The weird vibes begin to dissipate, and the silence of the night slowly returns. Moments pass without any further disturbances. Ryder's comfort level rises, and he almost passes back into La La Land. The tranquility is soon interrupted by a low droning sound echoing in from outside. His eyes pop open, and he spots a strange, faint glow coming from his yard.

"What the heck is that?"

The weird illumination pulsates brighter, the droning gets more intense and unearthly. It doesn't seem to be a manmade phenomenon; it appears eerie and unnatural. The creepiness shudders his entire body. He wishes he could stay safely under the covers but realizes that something truly bizarre is happening.

A strange energy lures him back to the window to do further surveillance, walking on tiptoes. He stops like a statue in mid-tip for a few pulsing heartbeats, wondering whether he should jump back in bed and forget the whole thing. He forces himself to continue, dropping to his hands and knees so whatever is out there can't see him.

"Ow. Oww. Owww." he mumbles as softly as possible as he kneels on the sharp corners of plastic video game cartridges.

"Note to self: clean your damn room already."

When Ryder finally peers over the ledge, his eyes bulge and his jaw drops. Like a caveman seeing fire for the first time. Twenty yards from the window, in the center of his backyard, is a vibrating radiance, glimmering intermittently. It reflects brightly and dimly off his face. His expression intensifies with every pulse. The drone is coming from the light, resonating louder, softer, then louder again. A bizarre simultaneous throbbing of light and sound. Almost resembling the heartbeat of some paranormal creature. It develops into a tormented moan. He is understandably shocked at first, shivering in fear. That quickly melts into a state of awe.

It is a formless supernatural presence, fluctuating between bluish grey and blood red. The phenomenon gets brighter and more vociferous with each pulse. It metamorphoses from an intangible glow into a corporeal presence. Almost as if it were a type of bizarre life form struggling to force its own birth. Gradually, the entity begins to mold itself into a physical shape, every throb giving it a clearer definition. Ryder is stunned as the top melds into a human face. The lower section forms into arms and a torso, connected to a long trail of blurriness instead of legs. The drone evolves into a humanoid shrieking. As if a teenage girl is crying to him from another dimension. Somehow, someway, the apparition is developing into a ghostly figure.

Ryder is in a nightmare state, as frightened and fascinated as he has ever been. His eyes, at first open wide with amazement, now have to squint from the sheer brilliance of the entity. He tries to run but is frozen stiff, his fingers vise-gripped onto the windowsill to stop himself from trembling.

"What the frick is that?" he whispers.

He checks around for other witnesses. Someone has to be hearing these blood-curdling squeals. Yet the area is vacant. The phantasm continues to swell and shriek, unable to burst free of its otherworldly dimension. It screams morosely, desperately wanting to evolve, but can't quite erupt. Its urgency, at last, gives Ryder the courage to speak.

"What are you? What do you want?"

But it cannot answer. It seems to realize that all its tenacious efforts to enter reality will never succeed. It circles repeatedly, almost in a tantrum. The spinning accelerates, a tornado gyrating with such intense energy that it corkscrews itself right into the earth and disappears.

Ryder is still petrified, barely breathing, kneeling there for an eternity. As he pushes himself away from the window, his body almost goes into a seizure; panting, sweating, and shaking. He crawls like a drunken monkey towards the bed, unconsciously crunching expensive games and slicing up his knees. He looks at his watch again and can't believe his eyes.

"2:13."

Ryder is thoroughly shell-shocked. That was only two minutes? He thought it lasted for two hours. The nightmare looks to be over, and his mind begins to recover. His pulse slows closer to normal. But just as the bed is within reach, he jumps away in horror. The glow has suddenly reappeared underneath it, emerging from the carpet. He rolls away, terrified.

"Aw, no way. No way. No way!"

The ferocity of the glow escalates. It gets more brilliant and fervent, then blazes right up through the mattress. Ryder slams himself against the wall, panic-stricken. The specter suspends itself in midair, and the image starts to form through the glimmering haze. It is a face of a young girl close to Ryder's age. A face so beautiful, he could just imagine it in a dream. A wondrous combination of sweetness and sexiness that he thought only Hollywood CGI could create. She hovers over the bed, glaring down at Ryder with unfathomable desperation. She tries frantically to communicate but is just able to utter short, wretched shrieks. Finally, after gathering all her strength, she does speak, in a despondent supernatural wail.

"Save me."

Ryder thought he was in a life-threatening situation. He is stunned to learn the ghost came here for help. She tries to communicate further but can't force out the words.

"Save you from what?"

Frustrated and running out of her unearthly energy, she screams out one last ear-splitting squeal. Then she spins herself right into the mattress, down into the floor, and vanishes.

Ryder keeps himself pinned into the corner of his room, exhausted. He gasps for air as if he were being strangled by a serial killer. He burns every ounce of his strength simply to keep himself from passing out. He stays there for the longest time, trying to comprehend what had just happened. Wondering if he will ever truly be sane again. How can he ever describe this to anyone? He pictures his parents dragging him to the basement and lacing him up into a homemade straitjacket. And shoving him into a makeshift padded cell they had built specifically for him. Never to see the light of day again.

Ryder finally gathers up enough courage to crawl to the bed. Still terrified, he compels himself to rip the blankets off and pat down the mattress. Like a cop searching for a dangerous suspect, he has to make sure the ghost is really gone. He leans over and cautiously takes hold of the dust ruffle along the floor-line, his fingers shaking as if it's 20 degrees below zero. He closes his eyes and grits his teeth, then rips the dust ruffle up to check under the bed for wailing phantasms.

"Yaaahh," he screams in an irrational attempt to scare away any lingering spirits. Then snickers because nothing is there except a dusty assortment of shoes and The Enchanted Pile of Lost Laundry. Ryder is relieved and freaked out at the same time. You hear about people getting abducted and anal probed by aliens all the time. No one ever mentions what the poor victims do with all the pent-up energy after such a close encounter. A battle-tested Marine would have hard time recovering from what happened to this poor teenager. His body shivers down to its very core.

He begins to decompress. The freakish thoughts storming around in his head settle themselves down. Why haven't his parents burst through his door, screaming about all the freakish sights and sounds? They've bitched at him before for merely farting too loud. Wait, he thought, what if the phantasm emerges in their room? What if she gets violent and attacks them while they sleep? They've never been the easygoing overseers he always wished they would be. But at this crucial moment of his life, he realizes his love for his mother and father is far greater than he ever understood.

Ryder knew that relating any version of recent events to them will make him sound like a babbling lunatic. The ghost may be homicidal, so he has to warn them. He struggles to get to his feet, but his legs are as rubbery and shaky as the sex toy he once found hidden in his mom's dresser drawer. He crumples to the floor, an outdoor Halloween ghost deflating into the grass. He resorts to crawling along the rug, a man dying of thirst and dragging himself across the desert, ultimately reaching their open doorway.

"Mom... Dad..." Ryder whispers, his voice too weak to be heard.

They're spooning as they snooze, which grosses him out a little. But they're safe and secure. Although the ghost scared the poop emojis out of him, it didn't physically harm him. His guts tell him they are safe for the night. The power in his battery has been depleted, and his vision darkens like a failing flashlight. His head sinks into the thick blue carpeting, and he falls asleep by the door as if a guard dog.

Hours have passed. Sunlight streams through the open window shades. His Mother, still attractive even with no makeup and her hair in curlers, returns from making breakfast to find her lone child Ryder still out of it on the floor.

"Well, at least he's not drunk or wasted, just weird and lazy," she thinks to herself. Mom winds up her dainty foot and gives him a swift kick in the butt, trying to awaken him from his coma-like state.

"Ryder. Ry—der. Wake your ass up, ya bum."

He doesn't even flinch. Exasperated, she bends over and shakes him into consciousness. His eyes open slowly, with a blank, wandering stare, as if he doesn't know where he's at.

"Why the hell are you sleeping on the floor?" his mom questions.

Suddenly, Ryder springs to his knees, scanning every corner of the room, still frightened and wary.

"What is wrong with you? I nearly broke my neck tripping over you when I got up this morning." she continues. Ryder is pale and trembling, worried that the wraith will return, and grabs his mom by the leg so tight that it cuts off her circulation. Exasperated, she tries to free herself from his unwanted embrace, only to end up dragging his ass comically around the carpet like a dog with worms.

"Let go of me, or I'll mop the kitchen with you. Let go." Exasperated, she punts him away, disgusted with his clinginess. "Are you deaf or something? Didn't you hear our alarm go off earlier? That thing is so loud it could wake the dead."

"Mom, I --"

"What?"

Ryder makes a vain attempt, still too groggy and freaked out. He can't put his overanxious thoughts into intelligible sentences yet. And his mom looks far too busy and annoyed to wait for an answer.

"Get your lazy butt up and take a shower for school. I don't know what kind of trouble you've gotten yourself into, but tenth grade awaits."

Ryder tries to explain again, but just sputters out incoherent mumbling.

"No excuses. Get going."

His mom is mortified. Ryder resembles a homeless mutt curled on the floor that way. She rolls her eyes, scornfully shakes her head at him, and storms out. Ryder wracks his brain for a rational story to warn her with. He draws a complete blank. How do you explain the unexplainable? To your mother?

"Mom. Come back," he laments.

She is too far away to hear him. He gives up and flounders to the floor with an angry curse as if his favorite team had just lost the Championship. He lies there wondering if the whole thing may have been night terrors. Or something psychologically explainable. Normal people have reported seeing UFOs and Bigfoot and the Loch Ness Monster. This made those legends downright plausible. Maybe a creep at school had roofied his Monster Mango Loco during lunchtime? He curls up in the fetal position, utterly drained. He is sore and exhausted from his unearthly encounter mere hours before and can't muster the energy to face the day. But his mom is tracking his every move from the kitchen with her parental radar.

"RYDER. If you're not in that shower in ten seconds, I'm calling your father." his mother yells, blindly perceiving that her son is still not getting ready. His young life flashes before his eyes, and the violent ending did not look fun. Ryder stretches desperately for the doorknob and uses it to pull himself up to his feet. Stumbling to the nearest rear window, he spies over the entire yard, hoping to find proof that he isn't insane. Not a trace of evidence.

He struggles to the bathroom and stares into the mirror. His eyes look different, as if he is gazing into the soul of a psycho. He pounds the back of his head against the opposite wall, trying to knock some sense back into his skull.

"It didn't happen. It couldn't have. It was only a dream."

He opens his eyes and stares at his reflection. He needs to be honest with himself. It did happen.

"There has to be a reasonable explanation."

Ryder is so tired he needs his arm to hold himself up at the vanity. He brushes his teeth in a vague attempt to get ready. Foam drools down his chin, giving him the look of a rabid dog.

"Yeah, that I'm a complete nut job."

On the other side of the house, it's just another day for his mom. She is racing around trying to eat while she's still cooking, cleaning the counters while loading the dishwasher, and getting her son ready for another day of school.

"Ryder, you have 3 seconds to get in here."

Ryder trudges in as if he is hobbling to Mount Doom instead of simply heading to school. Dragging his feet and moaning while still half-dressed. His mom snarls and snaps him on the butt with a damp dishtowel.

"What is the matter with you today?"

"Mom, I had a bad drea…"

Ryder catches his last word before it squeaks out. But Mom has heard enough.

"You had a bad what?"

He tries to switch game plans.

"I... I had a bad stomachache last night. It still hurts."

"Ryder, I don't know what mess you're in at school, just don't try to weasel your way out of it."

"No, it's just..."

"You're really in big trouble if I hear another word."

Sensing it's hopeless, he finishes buttoning his shirt. Mom slides his breakfast plate across the long kitchen table perfectly in front of her son, better than an Old West bartender whipping a beer along the bar.

"Now eat this fast, your bus should be here soon."

"Where's Dad?"

"He already left for work. And you're going to school. End of discussion."

Ryder mushes the scrambled eggs and sausage around on his plate. His stomach feels as if he just went ten rounds in The Octagon. And the thought of eating anything made him want to run for the Pepto. Crazy thoughts and explanations for last night's paranormal experience skittered around the inside of his skull like moths bouncing around a bug zapper.

"Mom?" Ryder interjected meekly.

"WHAT?" she answers angrily.

"Did you and Dad do a lot of drugs before I was born?"

His Mom's jaw drops, as does her plate, crashing and splattering across the floor. She explodes with a long barrage of language not suitable for younger viewers. Ryder stumbles from his chair and barrels for the door. He eases the door closed behind him so only the final click of the lock is audible.

The fresh breeze and blazing hot sunshine outside ease the turmoil he felt raging inside. They help him feel ever-so-slightly back to normal. The bus hadn't arrived yet, so he flops on the front porch like a bummed-out druggie. Maybe he is crazy. Could that be the reason his life was such a mess? He read that depressed people make dumbass mistakes, subconsciously yet deliberately, so they get fed up with everything and end it all. Maybe he is a Maniac Depressive? Maybe his life is already a giant snowball rolling downhill with a tree dead ahead.

"NO. I'm too young to give up." He straightens up and shakes away any stupid thoughts. Somehow, he has to prove last night's insanity isn't a schizophrenic episode.

"There's gotta be a way I can prove it happened."

Ryder jumps to his feet and runs around to the rear of the house. He searches the area where he first saw the apparition. A strange substance covers the grass at the very spot. He leans over and warily touches it. Clear gelatinous liquid the consistency of thick maple syrup. Still chilly despite the hot weather. It grosses him out, and he tries to shake it off his hand and wipes the rest away on the grass.

"Bleah. Nose jam."

It is spread across a snail trail along the lawn. His eyes follow it glistening in the sunshine all the way back to his bedroom window. He pumps his fist into the air and smiles.

"Yes. I knew it wasn't a dream."

So, the ghost really did appear. He isn't a total whack job. He can grow up, move away, and try to forget it ever occurred. Then he notices the trail also continues in the opposite direction, leading away from the house. He runs along for fifty feet or so till the gooey path ends right at the railroad tracks. There is even a large patch spread across the rail. Ryder never saw her travel that far away from his house. Did she return after he passed out? Is she an evil phantom trying to cause a train crash?

OMG. Phantoms causing train wrecks. If he ever tried to explain this to the kids at school, they would relegate him to the nerd table in the lunchroom forever. They would mold the tinfoil from all the Ding Dongs and Ho Ho's in their lunch bags and force him to wear it like a hat. Squeaky brakes and a loud beep from out front signals his school bus has arrived. He shrugs his shoulders and reluctantly heads off.

The room is jammed with rows of teenagers, some jocks, some freaks, and a lot of preppy rappers. They google on their laptops or swipe around on their phones. Miss Yaguchi, their pretty young Asian teacher, reads from an oversized textbook. Ryder is in the last row with his alphabetical best friends, seated by their last names. Jason, with designs etched into the sides of his buzz-cut hairline, is a big, tough kid with a big, fat mouth, and sits to his right, lording over everyone like the King of the Class. Brett, a stylish Ladies Man wannabe, sits to his left, working his charming bastard routine for any female who will listen.

Directly in front of them sit two girls. Nicole is a tall blond who acts as if she's God's Gift to teenage boys and male schoolteachers. She constantly wears overly expensive jewelry to correspond with her overly smug attitude. And Emma, a petite redhead who is always giggling, mostly at other people's misfortunes. She's been blessed with precociously large breasts, which match her exceedingly large nasty streak.

They can see the teacher is preoccupied, so they whisper back and forth, giggling and making cruel comments mocking the less fortunate-looking students. Jason and Brett notice Ryder is in a weird mood, which activates the macho bullshit segment of their brains. They shove him around and punch him in the arms. Ryder swats their hands away, tired of their hazing.

"Leave me alone," he mutters.

Everyone in the crew gives him the evil eye. He is now their target of wrath for the day.

"Looks like something crawled up Ryder's butt this morning," Nicole says.

"Yeah, dude, you're starting to turn into a real closet case," Jason says.

"Something really weird happened to me in bed last night," Ryder answers, instantly regretting it.

"Yeah, they're called nocturnal emissions." Emma jokes.

The crew of misfits chuckles quietly so the teacher can't hear, and high-five Emma in honor of her quick jab.

"Good one, Emma," Brett says.

Ryder is still trying to explain the events of the night before. Neither Brett nor Jason will listen, rattling on with meaningless bullshit. His senses overload and he backhands both of them at the same time.

"No, guys, really… listen,"

They stop immediately, and Jason stares him down.

"You better have cancer or something, cuz if you don't, I'm gonna beat you to death myself."

"I'm trying to tell you what happened. This strange light woke me up."

"Yeah, the light from Pornhub on your laptop." Emma jokes, drawing muted chuckles from her schoolmates.

"No, c'mon, guys. There was a weird light, and it was making this crazy sound."

"Ryder, the tracks are right behind your house." Jason points out. "It is probably some new kind of train equipment."

"No. I saw what it was. It was some kind of… ghost."

All four of Ryder's friends go dead silent. They were merely teasing him before. Now they're gaping at him as if he graduated from Class Clown to Town Idjit.

"I know it sounds psycho, but…"

"Ryder, we don't wanna hear about any of your dweeby dreams," Jason says angrily.

"Maybe if you were dreaming about Ariana Grande." Brett states.

"Now that's a different story," Jason agrees.

"Screw you guys."

Jason and Brett take offense and treat him as their own personal punching bag. Ryder tries to protect himself and fight back at the same time. He swings wildly at both of them, eyes shut tight, holding his head low so he doesn't catch a swat in the face. Emma and Nicole notice the teacher is closing her book and might glance up and catch them in the act. They warn Jason and Brett by tapping them on their shoulders, but not Ryder. They laugh and stop fighting, leaving Ryder to continue the battle alone.

Miss Yaguchi looks up and sees Ryder flailing punches at both of his buddies, who try to act as if they are as surprised by his actions as she is. He stops after realizing that they aren't punching him anymore. He warily lifts his face, squinting and flinching, still expecting a few fists to fly at him. What he does see is the teacher and his classmates watching him like he's the funniest new video on Tiktok. The entire room bursts into uproarious laughter. But not Miss Yaguchi.

"Ryder, what on earth are you doing?"

"I... uh... well... um,"

He is caught with his proverbial pants down and has no excuses. He slumps in his chair, red-faced, burying his face into his arms folded on the desk. Miss Yaguchi is ready to read him the riot act when there is a knock at the door, saving him even more public humiliation.

"Yes, come in," she says.

"Phew," Ryder exclaims, sighing in relief over this reprieve.

"You scabbed out, bitch." Jason says.

The door squeaks open, and a middle-aged woman enters. It's the principal's receptionist, Mrs. Blakely, a middle-aged former teacher. She changed jobs in order to stay as far away from crazy kids as possible while still keeping her pension.

"She's here. Miss Yaguchi." Mrs. Blakely says.

"Alright, bring her in."

Blakely walks out to the hall and ushers in a young girl.

"Class, we have a new student. Let's welcome Tajah Porter."

Ryder is still wiping the sweat from his brow when his expression turns from embarrassment into devastating shock. The new girl turns around to face her new schoolmates. She is

75

unmistakably the ghostly figure from the night before. He is so astonished that he forgets that he's in the middle of a classroom. He absent-mindedly leaps to his feet, points at the new student, and yells.

"Holy crap. It's her. It's… the ghost."

The silence is deafening. The eyes of the whole tenth grade zeroed in on Ryder. Mrs. Blakely lets out a startled yelp, her dentures slipping halfway out of her mouth. The entire class erupts with the laughter of a sitcom audience. They laugh harder than any other schoolroom ever did before. But his teacher doesn't even crack a smile. She is genuinely concerned with Ryder's bizarre antics.

"Ryder, are you on any medications?"

"Yeah, Ryder, did you bring enough to share with the rest of the class?" Nicole jokes.

"Dude, the last train to Psychotown leaves at 3… be on it." Brett declares.

Miss Yaguchi, exasperated, turns to the receptionist.

"Mrs. Blakely, can you please watch my students for a while?"

The stunned woman can't even answer, simply nods yes.

"Ryder, get up here. We're going to have a talk with the principal." He grudgingly rises and walks The Green Mile between desks with his chin in his chest, utterly humiliated.

"Dead Man Walking," Emma yells, to everybody's amusement.

The trip to the doorway takes an eternity. As he stumbles along, he peers at the many faces of his fellow students from his peripheral vision. They are either blustery red from laughing or staring at him like he's a leprous maniac.

As he approaches Tajah, she gives Ryder an odd gaze, as if she knows him from somewhere. Then her eyes pop open, as if a tiny bomb went off in her brain. She does recognize him. Before she can react, Miss Yaguchi interrupts.

"Tajah, we'll figure out the seating arrangements later. For right now, take Ryder's desk."

"Okay," she answers, still gazing at Ryder. She walks to the back of the room and sits between Jason and Brett, while Miss Yaguchi stares at her troubled student with deep concern.

"Okay, young man, come with me."

Inside the principal's waiting room, Ryder is well beyond despondent, seriously thinking of hopping the next freight out of town. He slouches in his chair so far down that his butt is half off the seat. His teacher has already had a conference with the principal and returned to her pupils.

Mrs. Blakely nervously types away at her desk, giving him an occasional frightened glance. She keeps track of his every move, as if he is an escaped serial killer. Concerned, muffled voices can be heard through the glass door. It opens, and the principal, a balding pencil-pusher with a tendency to get overdramatic, leads Ryder's rattled mother out of the office.

"Mom."

"Don't you say a word,"

"We don't know if he's acting out for attention, or there are underlying causes for such erratic behavior." The principal says. "Please take him to a therapist immediately, or we won't allow him to finish the semester."

"I am so sorry. I'm going to get to the bottom of this." his mom replies.

"Mom, you have to…"

"Ryder, get your butt in the car. You have no idea how much trouble you're in."

His mom grabs him by the arm and drags him from the office like a misbehaving toddler who won't leave Chucky Cheese. She pushes him through the doorway to the parking lot.

"Mom, you have to listen to my side of the story."

She turns around and gets right in his face.

"No, you have to listen to my side of the story. I had to take a day off work to listen to some jackass tell me how it's my fault that my son is a schizo."

She pulls the keys from her purse and beeps the doors unlocked.

"Now, get in there."

They get in the car, buckle up, and screech out of the lot. His mom digs through her overcrowded glove compartment. Car repair bills and sunglasses fall onto Ryder's lap. She finds an old pack of cigarettes, slides one from the pack with her lips and fires it up.

"See what you did? You got me smoking again." Mom says.

"Mom, something weird did happen last night," Ryder says.

"Your principal tells me you have mental problems. Or you're on drugs. Or BOTH."

"I'm not crazy and I'm not on drugs."

She stops at a red light and turns to him.

"Then what in God's name is the matter with you?"

"I woke up last night and saw this…" he says.

His mother turns back to look where she's driving and blabs right over his attempted explanation.

"Now I have to call the freaking psychiatrist."

"Mom, will you please listen?"

His mother is clearly not in the listening mood. She drives more erratically than he's ever seen. Speeding, cutting other drivers off, running yellow lights. Eventually, she squeals the car onto their block and pulls into the driveway, nearly decapitating a garden gnome near the garage.

"Get in the house."

"But Mom, I want to show you…"

He stops short when he sees her angry scowl They walk into the house, and she slams the door shut.

"Get in your room and stay there."

He turns and mopes away.

Back at school, the buzz has died down and things have returned to near normal. Miss Yaguchi is again busy with her paperwork. So, Ryder's friends quietly interrogate the new kid. Tajah is the new center of attention.

"So Tajah, are you a fa... fa... fa... friendly ghost?" Emma asks in jest.

"Hey, how come I can't see through you? You feel pretty solid to me." Brett says, poking at different parts of her body. Tajah slaps his hand away.

"Touch me again, and you'll be the ghost around here."

Everyone snickers except Tajah, who still seems worried over Ryder's situation. Even though he is a complete stranger, she senses a strange connection to him, as if they are mystically linked.

"What's wrong with your friend?"

"Ryder? I dunno, he must be hitting the Ritalin and White Claw pretty hard." Emma jokes.

"I think he got a hold of Joe Rogan's personal stash of DMT or something," Nicole adds.

"He actually admitted that he saw a ghost?" Tajah asks.

"Screw Ryder. Let's talk about you, babe." Jason says.

"Yeah, you're so freakin' hot, it's spooky," Brett says.

"Let me describe the dream I'm gonna have about you tonight." Jason says.

"Back off, Jason, before you drool all over yourself." Nicole cuts in.

Tajah eyes spin cartoonishly, flustered by the guy's immature attempts at rapping on her.

"Do you think Ryder going to be okay?" Tajah continues.

"He's never been okay. He's a part-time nerd who just graduated into a full-time loser." Jason replies.

"I'm sure his mom kicked his skinny ass on the way home HAHAHA," Emma says.

"Well, I feel bad for him." Tajah sighs.

She's not even trying to conceal the troubled expression on her face. Brett can't handle the fact that her interest is centered on Ryder and not him. His fragile ego won't accept being friend-zoned so quickly. So, he tries working on a different strategy.

"Tajah, are you walking home with us?"

"Doesn't everybody go home on the bus?"

"Usually, but since you're new, we're gonna walk you around and show you the neighborhood," Jason adds.

"Yeah, show you the coolest spots to hang out," Nicole says.

"I can't, my mom is going to pick me up," Tajah responds.

"Bitch, nobody goes home with their Mommy unless they're 9 years old." Emma laughs.

They all taunt her with mocking glares of condescension. Tajah is stuck. There is no way to avoid the peer pressure without everybody thinking she's a huge wuss.

"Alright, alright," she says. "I'll text my mom and tell her I'm going home with you guys."

"Yeah, baby. Just cuz you're sitting in Ryder's seat doesn't mean you have to be a dweebazoid like he is." Jason exclaims.

"Yeah, the bus driver is cool. He won't report us." Emma says.

"Yeah, we'll get you home no problem," Brett says.

"We're not gonna do anything dangerous," Nicole smirks.

The four friends flash their most evil eyes and toxic smiles at each other. As if they have some devious plans in the works for her.

Ryder rolls around restlessly. He doubts he will ever be able to sack out on this crib ever again. A gentle knock comes on his door. His mom sneaks in as quietly as Santa on Christmas. He keeps his eyes shut, pretending to be asleep until he knows whether she is still pissed at him.

"Ryder. Are you awake?" she asks in a sweet, motherly tone that he can hardly recognize. Her mood swing signals it's safe to open his eyes, but he is still wary. Moms are the sneakiest of all relatives. She can snap at any second.

"Yeah, I'm awake," he whispers.

She walks in and sits softly at the edge of his bed. Her wild anger has subsided, replaced by the sincere Mom face he loved. Her hand reaches out, gently touching his cheek, eyes glowing with concern. Or maybe she is hoping to find a reason to sweep the whole escapade under the proverbial rug and avoid the embarrassing psychiatric appointment.

"Okay, what the heck did you see last night?" she asks.

He pops up like a bagel from the toaster, excited that someone will finally listen to what he has to say.

"Thanks, Mom. There is this weird light and a strange sound. C'mon, you hafta see this."

He takes her by the hand and leads her to the window. She scoffs in protest, but reluctantly follows along.

"Look."

His Mom pretends to search around yet doesn't see anything out of the ordinary. At first. Her face lights up when she spots the trail the ghost traveled over, which now has withered into a pathway of dead grass.

"What the...?"

Ryder grins with euphoria, as his mom's attitude suddenly falls from Defcon 5 to at least Defcon 3.

Back at school, the clock on the wall hits 2:00 P.M. The bell rings, and the entire class explodes from their seats and rushes for the door.

"Okay, don't forget your assignments. See everybody tomorrow." Miss Yaguchi shouts over the happy uproar. Tajah follows her new friends, who sneak around the corner and out a side exit to avoid the school bus. They sneak to the rear of the school

81

through a vacant gangway, keeping a wary eye out for security guards. Jason pulls open a loose section of fence and the gang race out like escaping prisoners. Straight for the railroad tracks.

Meanwhile, Ryder is finishing his convoluted version of what occurred the previous evening to his mom. He jabbers away and waves his arms around so wildly she understands why the faculty at school thought he needed therapy. But she is as deft as a card shark at the World Poker Championship and knows her son's tells. Though it's the most ridiculous story she ever heard, she can tell her son is not lying to her. Whatever happened, the previous evening, this is pretty much how Ryder remembers it. She forces a smile and gives him a leery yet heartfelt hug.

"Mom, I know it's unbelievable. I wasn't dreaming. Something killed that grass."

"Yeah, probably one of your delinquent friends," she answers.

"I'm telling you it was an actual…"

"Okay, okay. Please stop talking about ghosts. The neighbors will think you're a whacko."

"You don't think that do you, Mom?"

"Oh, no, you're a whacko. But you're my whacko," she says. "I'm stuck with you. Just remember, the next time magical spirits appear, do me a huge favor and shut your eyes."

Ryder is hurt by his mother's insensitive comments. At least she realizes that something weird really did happen. She wanders out of Ryder's room in a daze, wondering if shaking her head and rolling her eyes so often might cause a cerebral hemorrhage.

Now only a mile away from his house, Ryder's gang of misfit schoolmates are leading their raw recruit along the lonely stretch of tracks.

"This shortcut saves around five minutes," Emma tells Tajah.

"Otherwise, you would have to walk all the way around the factories," Brett adds. Tajah is still understandably nervous.

"You guys walk this way a lot?" she asks.

"Not too often, but because you're a noobie, we decided to give you our special tour," Jason replies.

They cackle strangely, and give each other weird stares, making Tajah even more uncomfortable. It's as if they have something diabolical planned for her. She fights the urge to run from her new classmates because this area is so unfamiliar to her. Fearful she would get herself lost in an unfamiliar urban maze. Following these punks on the uneven prairie makes her stumble a bit. Mosquitos buzz at her ears. She worries whether the grass would stain her brand new, first-day-at-school kicks. The hot sun and the strange behavior of this motley crew bring droplets of sweat cascading down every part of her body.

Suddenly, a deafening whistle blares behind them. A train is approaching just a thousand feet behind. It gets louder. The massive power of the engine getting nearer frightens Tajah. Nervous, she moved further away from the tracks. To her amazement, the others walk even closer.

"We'd better move away from here," she says.

"Why? It's only a train," Jason says.

"Yeah, didn't they have trains where you used to live?" Emma mocks.

"Yes. We stayed the hell away from them."

The roaring engine barrels past with frightening power. Tajah stares in disbelief as these four freaks wander around mere inches from the metallic monster. Suddenly, Jason starts running alongside it. Tajah is baffled, thinking he must be trying to race it. Instead, he grabs hold of a rung from the ladder of a boxcar and leaps aboard with an insane gleam in his eyes. Tajah is stunned.

"Yeah, baby," Jason screams at the top of his lungs. He hangs on with one hand and pumps his free fist into the air repeatedly as his friends cheer him on. They all run along for a block or so, till he had his fill of lunacy for the day and leaps off. He body rolls safely onto a grassy knoll as if he is taking a casual stroll. The others run up, applauding him as he bounces to his feet. He points forward with authority, like a football player who just made a first down.

"That was a blast," Jason yells.

"You rock, Jason." Nicole squeals, embracing him as a conquering hero.

"That was so bitchin'." Emma joins in, hugging him as well.

"My turn," Brett shouts. He gallops alongside another boxcar, measuring how high and fast he will have to jump. Seeing his chance, he leaps up, snatches hold of a ladder rung, and drags himself up. The others scream their approval. Not Tajah, though. Nothing she has ever experienced in her short life has scared her nearly this much.

"C'mon, Tajah. Jump on." Brett hollers. Tajah is freaked out by their demented game.

"I'm not doing that," she exclaims.

"C'mon, Tajah. It's your initiation into our gang." Nicole yells.

"Follow us, Taj," Emma hollers.

Nicole and Emma join Brett, leaping onto the train. The gang hangs off the cars with one hand, shouting over the uproar of the engines.

"It's so easy. Don't be such a wuss." Nicole screams.

"Jump on or be a loser for the rest of high school." Emma jeers at her.

Tajah wants to run from these crazy thugs as fast as she can. It's just that she has no idea which way to run. The school is lost in the vague distance. Her phone can't even pick up one bar of a signal. She'd be lost in an unfamiliar area, with no idea how to get home. The others jump and roll off the train like seasoned hobos, making it look so easy. They surround her, taunt her, pressure her to make the treacherous leap.

"Tajah. Tajah. Tajah." they chant. She refuses to budge. Jason angrily storms up right in her face.

"Get on the fucking train," he screams with an insane grimace. Ryder seeing a ghost seemed so normal compared to these lunatics. Now she is more afraid of Jason and the others than she is of the train. She gazes at the ten thousand tons of screeching, graffiti-covered metal, gulps down her fear, and takes off running.

"Yeah." her four future ex-classmates holler in unison.

Tajah races alongside, agonizing over when she should attempt a leap at the ladder. She takes a swipe at one rung but misses. She waits anxiously for the next boxcar with a ladder. As it reaches her, she grabs hold and leaps on.

"Awright, Tajah," Jason yells.

"Way to go, girl," Emma screams.

Tajah is terrified yet thrilled. The rush of doing something so out of character gives her a rush of excitement. Adrenaline loves danger. Her blushing cheeks and ear-to-ear grin belie the fear still churning inside. She waves at her new gang triumphantly, the new Queen of the Rails. Yet the rattling is too unnerving, the noise too unbearable. She tries to jump off, but her jean jacket gets caught up on the rusty metal. Her fingers clutch desperately for something to grab hold of, as she is left hanging by the torn denim.

The girls scream as they run alongside, wanting to help, yet paralyzed with fear. Jason and Brett simply stop running, angry that Tajah is now in danger and worried about what their parents are going to think. She desperately attempts to free herself, although she knows she is destined to drop right under the deadly wheels of the train.

Meanwhile, Ryder is playing video games in his room. After living his entire life near the tracks, his hearing is fine-tuned, and he can hear screaming over the blaring train. He leaps to his window and sees Tajah frozen to the boxcar. Realizing he can't waste time running for the door, he raises the window screen and barrels out. His feet fly at light speed towards the passing freight, while his punk-ass friends who caused the whole ordeal wander uselessly behind. Ryder sprints to rescue a girl he only knows as a nightmare. By the time he reaches her, she's sobbing uncontrollably.

"I'm gonna pull you away," he screams out.

Tajah is too frightened to jump, or even speak. She can only shake her head to say "no".

"Tajah, you have to let go. This train heads out of town at full speed." Ryder hollers. He knows once this thing reaches a certain point it speeds up to 80 miles an hour. Tajah is still unwilling, clinging to the rungs of the ladder and refusing to let go. But when it takes a turn around a large factory, the group spots a tunnel looming ominously ahead. The train will be entering the pitch-black cave in less than a minute, leaving her dangling helplessly in the shadows.

"Tajah, I got you," Ryder yells with authority. His attitude and actions make him feel like a man for the first time. Tajah is so terrified her brain won't let her think straight. She is caught up in the most horrible moment of her young life, and her next choice might tragically end it. So, Ryder decides for her.

"Tajah, I'm going to grab you. You have to let go or we'll both die."

Sweating and running out of energy as they barrel closer to the tunnel, Ryder makes his move. He snatches Tajah by the waist and drags her away with all his strength. The jacket rips away, but before she falls to a brutal death under the lethal wheels, Ryder pulls her to safety.

He carries her away, marching as a conquering hero for a few steps, then stumbles to the ground. They spin down an incline together, ending up face to face. Their eyes meet with an instant connection. Tajah is in shock. Ryder is amazed his plan worked. Fate has stopped them so close together, their lips almost touch. They are about to kiss until the other four teens rush up and interrupt.

"Are you guys okay?" Nicole asks.

"I'm fine," Ryder replies. Jason and Brett pull the pair to their feet, swatting at their backs, dusting them off and congratulating them simultaneously.

"Man, that was freaking insane." Jason hollers.

"Ryder, dude, you saved her life." Emma exclaims.

"Yeah, you saved ghost girl's life." Nicole laughs.

The entire experience sinks in. Ryder stares at his watch. It's broken right at 2:11.

"2:11. The exact time I saw the ghost last night. I mean… when I saw you," he says. Tajah looks at her watch, and her face changes from shock to amazement. She holds it wrist to wrist next to Ryder's. They are both broken exactly at 2:11. The whole gang freaks out at the bizarre coincidence.

"I dreamt about you last night, too," Tajah confesses. "Well, it wasn't a dream… this was way more real. I don't remember the train or anything else, just that I reached out to you for help. And you saved my life."

Tajah finally explodes, unable to hold back her emotions any longer, kissing him passionately again and again. She squeezes him as tightly as the rungs of the train, hanging on for dear life. When she curls up in his arms, something magical transforms her beating heart. More than just pheromones or the thrill of danger. He is her safety net, her security blanket. He would always protect her.

Ryder feels love as a tangible presence in his life. Not just something he has to imagine from a song or a movie. They gaze into each other's eyes, sensing some type of supernatural force has brought them together. Even though they're strangers, they have a symbiotic relationship much deeper and stronger than any fleeting high school crush.

The train jumpers scatter as blaring sounds erupt from across the field. Several railroad security cars speed towards them across the prairie, sirens wailing, lights flashing. They know they're all in a huge jam. Except for Tajah and Ryder. They'll be able to handle whatever life throws at them from now on.